Another shot cracked through the air. It was coming from the bar, and whoever fired it was nowhere to be seen. Even so, they were a good enough shot to hit one of the gunmen in the leg and drop him straight to the floor.

"Jesus!" the scarred man grunted.

"There must be more of 'em, Jeff!"

Looking over to the gunman who'd said that, the scarred man shook his head. "One of 'em got lucky is all."

As if in direct response to that, another shot was fired. This one caught the other gunman at the scarred man's side and dropped him with a wound similar to the one that had put the first one onto the floor.

Jeff squinted and leaned toward the bar. "Son of a bitch is shooting through the bar. This might just be the real Gunsmith after all."

Both gunmen look toward Jeff as if the rest of the saloon no longer mattered.

"What?" they asked in unison.

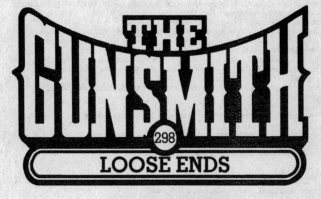

THE GUNSMITH

298

LOOSE ENDS

J. R. ROBERTS

JOVE BOOKS, NEW YORK

THE BERKLEY PUBLISHING GROUP
Published by the Penguin Group
Penguin Group (USA) Inc.
375 Hudson Street, New York, New York 10014, USA
Penguin Group (Canada), 90 Eglinton Avenue East, Suite 700, Toronto, Ontario M4P 2Y3, Canada
(a division of Pearson Penguin Canada Inc.)
Penguin Books Ltd., 80 Strand, London WC2R 0RL, England
Penguin Group Ireland, 25 St. Stephen's Green, Dublin 2, Ireland (a division of Penguin Books Ltd.)
Penguin Group (Australia), 250 Camberwell Road, Camberwell, Victoria 3124, Australia
(a division of Pearson Australia Group Pty. Ltd.)
Penguin Books India Pvt. Ltd., 11 Community Centre, Panchsheel Park, New Delhi—110 017, India
Penguin Group (NZ), Cnr. Airborne and Rosedale Roads, Albany, Auckland 1310, New Zealand
(a division of Pearson New Zealand Ltd.)
Penguin Books (South Africa) (Pty.) Ltd., 24 Sturdee Avenue, Rosebank, Johannesburg 2196,
South Africa

Penguin Books Ltd., Registered Offices: 80 Strand, London WC2R 0RL, England

This is a work of fiction. Names, characters, places, and incidents either are the product of the author's imagination or are used fictitiously, and any resemblance to actual persons, living or dead, business establishments, events, or locales is entirely coincidental.

LOOSE ENDS

A Jove Book / published by arrangement with the author

PRINTING HISTORY
Jove edition / October 2006

Copyright © 2006 by Robert J. Randisi.

ISBN: 0-515-14209-3

JOVE®
Jove Books are published by The Berkley Publishing Group,
a division of Penguin Group (USA) Inc.,
375 Hudson Street, New York, New York 10014.
JOVE is a registered trademark of Penguin Group (USA) Inc.
The "J" design is a trademark belonging to Penguin Group (USA) Inc.

PRINTED IN THE UNITED STATES OF AMERICA

10 9 8 7 6 5 4 3 2 1

ONE

The town was so small that the couple of folks living there didn't even bother building houses for themselves. Instead, they simply put up their businesses and slept in the back. The thought behind that was that they were saving money to allow the settlement to prosper, or they could pick up and leave fairly easily if it didn't.

Since the little general store was the only place to get supplies within fifty miles in any direction, it appeared as though the store and a few of the other businesses would do pretty well for themselves. One of the stores had even managed to attract an investor or two who knew well enough how scarce supplies were in that part of California.

Then again, a hundred investors wouldn't do the place any good if it couldn't stand up on its own through the rough times.

One of those trials faced by many businesses was in dealing with the trash who breezed in and tried to get a few things into their pockets without the intention of paying for them. The owner of the general store had developed a knack for spotting those thieves after the first week his doors had been opened. Since then, he'd come up with a few good ways of discouraging such behavior.

1

Ronald Moore was in his late forties and had a few gray hairs to show for it. His hands were thick with calluses, showing that he was no stranger to putting in a hard day's work. As the owner of the general store, he was also one of the founders of that small, sorry excuse for a nameless town. His eyes were normally friendly and warm. Lately, however, he'd learned to put an edge into his stare when a certain type of customer walked through his door.

Both of the men who were currently prowling up and down the two aisles of merchandise were just such customers.

The men were dirty, but no more so than anyone else who'd spent a good portion of his day in the saddle. They were armed, but that was also nothing particularly noteworthy. What caught Ronald's attention was the fact that neither of the men in his shop looked like they had the potential to be clean.

Both customers looked gritty by their very nature, and the guns they wore were obviously for more than shooting the occasional snake. Their eyes were narrowed and harsh. Apart from a short hello when they'd walked in, neither customer had said a word to Ronald. Instead, they whispered among themselves in short, clipped phrases.

"You sure I can't help you fellas with something?" Ronald asked.

One of the men glanced over as if the shop's owner was a gnat buzzing loudly in one ear. "No," he grumbled. "We're doing just fine."

The other man kept his eyes on Ronald for a few seconds more than his friend. As if sensing the apprehension building up in the store's owner, he walked over and plastered a smile onto his face. "Actually, there is something I'd like to ask."

"Ask away," Ronald said.

"I'd like to know how long you've been in business. We rode through here not too long ago and none of this was even built."

"We've been here for just under a year. Actually, just over half a year."

"Time flies, huh?"

"Yessir. It sure does."

"From what I hear, folks think this settlement's about to boom."

"We've got our hopes up," Ronald said. "It'd be a shame to pull up stakes after building our places up and sinking everything we've got into them. But, I suppose most men who own their own businesses think along those same lines."

"But not everyone's got the backing of men who can help them through the rough times. Ain't that so?"

Ronald's eyes narrowed a bit as the sinking feeling in the pit of his stomach returned. "What do you mean by that?"

When the customer who'd done most of the talking turned around, he didn't have to look far to find the other man who'd come in with him. The bigger fellow had sidled up right next to him and was also staring down the shop owner.

Neither man had drawn his gun just yet, but they kept their hands close enough to their holsters to put Ronald on his guard.

"I don't mean anything by it," the first customer replied. "All I meant to say was that good friends in high places are never a bad thing to have."

"No," Ronald replied cautiously. "I guess not. Now, was there anything I can help you find today?"

"What's the matter? Suddenly you don't seem to be enjoying my company."

Ronald shrugged.

Turning to his larger companion, the customer said, "What do you think, Hobbes? Is this place getting busy all of a sudden, or are we wearing out our welcome?"

Hobbes grinned and took a step toward Ronald. Just that little bit of motion was enough to make him seem to grow. Actually, it was more like a cobra straightening up while displaying a wide hood. The gleam in Hobbes's eyes wasn't too far from that found in a deadly snake.

"Seems like we're not welcome anymore," Hobbes said.

Ronald found himself shaking his head. "Not at all," he said while turning and walking back to the front counter where his shotgun was kept. "Jus let me know if either of you need anything."

"We do need something," the first customer said as he stalked over to the counter and leaned on it with both hands. "I'll start off with some new bedrolls and then I'll take a list of all your investors."

Ronald flinched as if some of those words had stung his eyes. "I've got the bedrolls, but . . . what was that last part?"

"You heard the man," Hobbes said as he walked around to Ronald's side of the counter. "We want to know who lent you the money to open up a shop in this stretch of empty fucking road."

"That kind of language isn't necessary." As he spoke, Ronald reached down to his shotgun. To his surprise, Hobbes bent down and snatched the gun from its hiding place and held it within his beefy hands.

As he glared over the counter, the first customer said, "And pulling a shotgun on a man just for asking a simple question isn't necessary either. What's the matter? Is this the way you treat all your prospective customers?"

"I know who you are," Ronald croaked.

"Is that so? Who am I, then?"

"You're Xander Prouse. Wanted for robbing those banks in Kansas, killing those folks on that stage from Tombstone and selling those poor Missouri girls to the savages."

Listening to that list of accusations, Prouse merely nodded. "You got most of that right. I just didn't know I was so famous around these parts."

"You blew up a bridge less than twenty miles from here. The law's been coming around asking if we seen you."

"And I suppose you'd tell right away now that you have?"

Ronald's eyes grew wide as saucers and he shook his head. "N-no, sir. I won't say a thing. If you want my money, take it. There's not much, but it's all yours."

"I'm not here to rob you," Prouse said. "I'm here to get some information. Now, unless you want to add murdering a shop owner to that list you memorized, I'd suggest you answer my question regarding those investors."

TWO

Clint hadn't been in California for an entire day before he knew he was being followed. It was a feeling that crept under his skin like an insect whose shell was made of ice. For men that weren't used to being followed, that chill was something easily overlooked. For Clint, however, it was that same chill that oftentimes meant the difference between life and death.

The feeling had made itself known as an itch in the back of his mind not long after he'd ridden over the state line. The more he rode, the colder that feeling got, until he was absolutely certain he was being watched. For some men, that might be considered twitchy or paranoid. Clint knew better than to write off such things, even when he couldn't figure out exactly where that feeling was coming from.

From the moment he felt it, Clint started looking over his shoulder. It was a kind of game as he snapped Eclipse's reins just to get the stallion running so he could look back and see as much open land as possible. Even when he saw nothing but open land, Clint knew he was missing something. He didn't doubt someone was watching him. That someone just had to be very good at their job.

Another day's ride and Clint was still playing the game. Finally, he headed for the first town he could reach and

7

rented a room inside a saloon. Clint normally preferred to stay in a hotel simply because it was quieter than sleeping around so many drunks and gamblers. This time, however, he used the saloon as cover.

Clint didn't even look at the name of the place. All that he cared about was that it was the biggest one of its kind in town and was therefore the biggest target. After wandering in and paying for his room, he dragged his saddlebags up the stairs and immediately looked for another way back down.

For a moment, Clint thought he might have to shimmy down a railing or even rush back down the main stairs. But he found a narrow set of stairs behind a door that he'd first thought was a closet. The saloon was busy enough for him to get downstairs without being noticed, and Clint sat down at the first card game he could find.

He tossed in enough cash to keep him playing and positioned himself so he could watch the front door. After that, all that was left to do was wait.

Wait and play with some of the worst gamblers he'd met in a good, long while.

Just over an hour later, Clint saw a thin figure covered in baggy clothes standing in the front doorway. Even though he couldn't see much more than that from where he was sitting, Clint just knew that was who he'd been waiting for.

The face of the person in the doorway was covered by an old hat with a brim encrusted with dirt. Light green eyes stared out from under that brim, taking in everyone standing at the bar.

"Can I help you with something?" the barkeep asked.

Since it was too late to slip past the bartender, the figure moved out of the doorway and got close enough so the next question didn't have to be shouted across the room. With one flip of a hand, the figure tipped back the floppy hat to reveal a face that was just pretty enough to catch the bartender off his guard.

"Oh," the bartender said with a start. "I didn't know you was a lady."

Despite the dirt covering her face and clothes, the woman was undeniably beautiful. Her dark brown hair was tied back and tucked under her collar. While the cut of her clothes was obviously intended for a man, she filled them out very nicely. It was only because of her large jacket that those curves weren't noticed immediately.

"What's the matter?" the woman asked with a subtle edge to her voice. "Don't you serve ladies here?"

The bartender was obviously flustered the longer he tried to think of what he wanted to say. "Sure we do. It's just that . . . I thought . . ."

Just then, a smile crossed the woman's face. "No need for all of that. You didn't step on anyone's toes."

"No offense, ma'am," the barkeep said after letting out a breath. "What can I get for you?"

"I'll take a whiskey as well as a bit of conversation."

"I can do my best on both accounts." Reaching for one of the bottles behind him, the bartender set a glass down in front of the woman and filled it with a brown liquid. "There's one. Now for the other."

"Do you know most everyone that comes through here?" she asked.

"More or less."

"Any new faces recently?"

"Like how recent?"

Putting on a thoughtful expression, the woman shrugged and said, "Like maybe today. Even the last few hours."

"Perhaps. You got anyone specific in mind?"

Like a shark that smelled fresh blood in the water, the woman could sense the barkeep was being wound slowly around her little finger. It was obvious in the way he leaned closer to her with every passing second and the way his voice softened the longer he talked to her. And, like any well-seasoned predator, the woman used everything at her disposal to bring him in.

"Maybe," she said.

The barkeep looked her up and down. Now that she was

closer, the woman was even more attractive than he'd first thought. She'd unbuttoned her jacket to put her gloves into an inner pocket. That way, the bartender could make out the impressive curves of her breasts. Even beneath the man's shirt she was wearing, her chest was large enough to put a little strain upon the buttons.

Her jeans hugged her hips just enough to show their feminine shape. From afar, she could have gone unnoticed. That was no longer the case now that she was close enough for the barkeep to get a better look. That effect was compounded whenever she shifted from one foot to another.

"Too bad you've already got someone in your sights," the barkeep said.

"He's just a friend of the family," she whispered while giving him a smirk that she knew most men found irresistible. "I saw his horse tied up outside."

Hope sprang right back into the barkeep's eyes. "Friend of the family, huh?"

"Nothing more than that."

"You got a name for me?"

"Adams."

Although he didn't say so right away, the barkeep recognized that name. He gave that much away by pausing at all before answering. "He might be here, but I'm not in the practice of breaking my customers' confidence."

"So he's a customer? Is he renting a room here?"

The barkeep winced as if he only just realized that he was being played like a fiddle. That wince grew even more as he turned away and quickly found someone else nearby who needed a drink.

Sensing the sudden shift in the atmosphere, the woman turned to get a look at what had caused the barkeep's sudden silence. She found it even quicker than she'd expected when she discovered Clint standing directly beside her.

"I am renting a room here," Clint said with a grin. "Who's asking?"

THREE

"You startled me," the woman said.

Clint kept his smile in place and took the spot next to her. "That was my intention."

"Well, that's not very polite."

"Really? And I suppose it's the height of politeness to follow a man across the state line?"

She put a surprised look on her face that was actually pretty good. If Clint hadn't known any better, he might have thought that she truly didn't know what he was talking about. But he did know better, and no amount of shifting on her feet could convince him otherwise.

"Perhaps you've mistaken me for someone else," she offered.

By now, the barkeep had mustered up the nerve to step back over to where Clint and the woman were talking. "I hope this isn't anything you need help with, ma'am."

Clint slowly looked over to the barkeep with an intensity that rooted the other man to the floor. "It's not. My name's Adams. I'm the friend of her family."

"Oh," the barkeep said with no small amount of relief. "Then I guess I'll leave you to your conversation."

"Thanks," the woman said. "That's real brave of you."

Clint leaned against the bar and tipped his hat back a ways on his head. It allowed her to see more of his face, while also taking away some of the hard edge to his appearance. "Since you already know who I am, why don't you tell me who you are?"

Since there was no way for her to get away from the conversation short of running from it, she straightened up and shifted her shoulders so the holster around her waist could be seen beneath her jacket. "I'm Lyssa Spencer."

"You say that like I should recognize the name."

"You might. Plenty of other people do."

"How might I have heard it?"

"I'm known for tracking men down. Some even say I'm the best."

"You're a bounty hunter?" Clint asked.

It was plain to see that she took offense to that. "No. I'm a tracker. Are you deaf?"

"All right, all right," Clint said while patting the air between them. "No need to get snippy. You're a tracker. Now, why are you tracking me?"

"I was paid to find you and bring you back to Colton."

"Who's Colton?"

"Not who. Where. It's a town in—"

Clint snapped his fingers and said, "That's right. It's a town right here in California. I don't believe I've ever been there."

"Well, that's about to change since you and me are headed back there as soon as possible."

"Are we, now? For someone who acts like they were nervous for me to know they were here, you seem awfully bold. Normally, I admire that quality in a person."

Truth be told, Clint liked the way Lyssa stood up to him and looked him straight in the eye when she spoke. There was a definite strength in her voice and body that was appealing all the way down to the animal level of Clint's brain.

Despite the challenge in her gaze and the subtle aggressive tilt in her head, it seemed that Lyssa knew firsthand how that sort of attraction felt.

She nodded a bit and replied, "You gave me a run for my money, Adams. That's something I admire in a man."

"Good to know I'm doing good so far."

"It's not often that I nearly have to give up on a job. Fact is, you were the first one to nearly give me the slip altogether." She picked up her drink and tilted it back. After some of the liquor had worked its way down her throat, she added, "Nearly."

Clint took a sip of the beer he'd ordered and leaned against the bar. Rather than say anything right then, he took a few moments to take a longer look at Lyssa. It was a practice that was much more important than some might have guessed.

It was a way to get a handle on someone, which wasn't yet affected by preferences or emotions. Like staring a man down from across a poker table, Clint allowed himself to get a real good impression of someone before they had a chance to swing his opinion one way or another.

Also, in Lyssa's case, taking a long look at her had its own set of advantages.

"You like what you see?" she asked.

Clint shrugged and looked over the bar at the shelves of bottles there. "So far. You sure don't seem like the normal type who tracks men down for a living."

"Is that because I'm a woman?"

"No. It's because you're good at what you do, but not too arrogant about it. I'd also peg you as the type who isn't afraid of using that gun you're carrying."

"I'd rather not if I can help it."

"And that tells me even more about you."

She smiled, sipped her drink and set the glass down. "Why do I suddenly feel like I'm the one that should be on my toes?"

"Aren't you always?" Clint asked.

"Right about now is when most men are either threaten-

ing me, trying to get away from me or trying to seduce me."
She gave Clint a good once-over and then smirked some
more. "I was told you were a cool drink of water."

"By the man that hired you?"

She nodded.

"And is that man about my height, with long hair and a
scar running across his chin?"

"No. How'd you come to that?"

"Turn around and see for yourself."

FOUR

A man walked straight up to the bar. He was about Clint's height, with long hair and a scar running across his chin. He also wore a gun on each hip and another strapped across his back. There were a couple other armed men keeping pace with him, but it was easy enough to see that the man with the scar was the leader of that pack.

"You know these fellas?" Clint asked in a voice just above a whisper.

Lyssa had already put her back to the bar and dropped her hand down to her gun. "Not personally, but I've seen them now and again."

"I'm guessing it wasn't a social call."

With a halfhearted chuckle, Lyssa shook her head and then turned to face the oncoming men.

"Well, well," the scarred man said. "Looks like we was meant to cross paths again, darlin'."

"I told you before to steer clear of me," Lyssa replied.

"Why would we do that? Not only did you bring us to the man we were after, but we also get to look at your pretty little. . ." As he spoke, he let his eyes wander slowly along the lines of Lyssa's breasts, stomach and legs. When he drifted back up to look into her eyes again, he grunted, "face."

"What's the matter?" Lyssa asked with blatant challenge in her voice. "You never seen a woman this close before? Maybe you should spend less time riding with your boyfriends here and pay some money for some female companionship."

"Or I could take whatever the hell I wanted."

"All right," Clint said as he felt the heat from Lyssa's blood coming to a boil. "You found us. Now what?"

The scarred man glanced slowly over to Clint and said, "Now you get to send a little message for us." With that, he snatched the gun from his holster and brought it up to aim at Clint. The men behind him followed suit and drew their own guns as well.

Clint didn't expect such drastic action, but that didn't mean he wasn't ready for it. The instant he saw the scarred man's hand close around his gun, Clint's muscles worked on their own accord.

The first thing Clint did was grab hold of Lyssa and pull her away from the other men. With his free hand, he drew his modified Colt and fired a shot. The gun roared and bucked against his palm, blasting the scarred man clean off his feet.

Although they were rattled at seeing the first man drop, the others who'd been on either side of the scarred man didn't abandon their spots. Instead, they held their ground and fired at Clint and Lyssa. Their bullets whipped through empty air and buried themselves into the bar as well as the wall behind it, since their targets were no longer in sight.

The scarred man's back had barely even hit the floor before he rolled to his side and jumped back to his feet. With his teeth clenched and blood pouring from the fresh wound in his ribs, he drew his second pistol and started pulling both triggers in quick succession.

Clint only saw her from the corner of his eye, but that was enough to see Lyssa jump over the bar like a deer in full stride sailing over a fallen log. He wasn't quite so graceful, but he managed to put the bar between himself and the gunmen as the lead filled the air like a hailstorm.

"Who the hell are these guys?" Clint snarled as he hunkered down behind the bar.

Lyssa held her pistol up to fire a few wild shots over the bar, but was stopped when Clint pulled her hand back down again. When she turned to glare at Clint, there was enough fire in her eyes to burn the whole saloon down.

"Answer my question before firing blind into a crowded room!" he said.

After taking a breath, she retracted her arm and winced as another volley of lead pounded into the bar. "I don't know who they are, but they've been following me for a while now."

"How long?"

"A few days. Maybe more, but that's when I saw they were tailing me."

"Tailing you while you were tailing me?" Clint asked.

She nodded reluctantly.

"Great," Clint said as he popped his head up to fire a quick shot at the closest gunman. "That's just great. And here I was starting to think you were one of the best trackers I've met in a while."

Grinning, Lyssa said, "Maybe the next best."

Clint had to laugh at a woman who would split hairs like that in the middle of a gunfight. Whether she was the best or next best, he surely couldn't doubt the fact she was gutsy as hell.

"Since we've got a quiet moment to talk," Clint said as a few more shots chewed into the bar and hissed over his head, "why don't you tell me what this message is?" Another round blasted apart the glass Lyssa had been drinking from and ricocheted off of a bracket on the wall. "Make it the short version."

Lyssa was about to answer, but the shots were getting closer by the second. Although the bar was thick enough to act as a good shield for a little while, it wasn't made of steel. More and more holes were appearing as the thick wood began to splinter.

"He might be wanting to get under someone's skin," she offered while peeking over the bar and firing a shot.

"By someone, you mean your employer."

"Yeah."

"What's his name?"

Wincing as a shot finally managed to come all the way through the thick wood of the bar, Lyssa spat out a single word that Clint would never have expected: "Earp."

FIVE

"You all right?" one of the other gunmen asked as they got a look at the scarred man.

Perhaps because the rest of him didn't look to be in much better shape, the bloody gash in the scarred man's side wasn't too out of place. It seemed even less serious as the man got to his feet and shook it off like it was nothing more than a splinter.

"I've had worse," the scarred man snarled. "Let's just finish what we came to do."

"They're still behind there."

"Then flush them out of there! We ain't got enough bullets to chip away that whole fucking bar."

Just then, another shot cracked through the air. What separated this from the rest was that it wasn't being fired wildly and it wasn't coming toward the bar. It was coming from the bar, and whoever had fired it was nowhere to be seen. Even so, they were a good enough shot to hit one of the gunmen in the leg and drop him straight to the floor.

"Jesus!" the scarred man grunted.

"There must be more of 'em, Jeff!"

Looking over to the gunman who'd said that, the scarred man shook his head. "One of 'em just got lucky is all."

As if in direct response to that, another shot was fired. This one caught the other gunman at the scarred man's side and dropped him with a wound similar to the one that had put the first one onto the floor.

Jeff squinted and leaned toward the bar. A smile crossed his scarred face as he nodded. "Son of a bitch is shooting through the bar. This might just be the real Gunsmith after all."

Both gunmen on the floor looked toward Jeff as if the rest of the saloon no longer mattered. "What?" they both asked in unison.

But Jeff had already moved on to shove over the nearest table and squat down behind it. He still had a pistol in each hand and leaned out to fire both of them at the bar. Although plenty of sound and fury exploded from his twin barrels, the only real effect he had was in sending more splinters into the air.

Behind the bar, Clint kept his hand steady while sighting along the top of his Colt's barrel. Since the pistol was poking through a large crack that had been put into the bar, he needed every bit of concentration he could muster if he was going to aim through that same crack.

"Did you say Earp was the name of the man who hired you?" Clint asked after squeezing off his last round and then pulling his Colt back to reload.

But Lyssa was already too far away to hear and too distracted to answer as she crept along the length of the bar so she could get a better angle from which to shoot. She stood up and emptied her pistol with a smile on her face, buying Clint enough time to finish reloading and snap his cylinder shut.

Sucking in a deep breath, Clint sprung to his feet and fired a few quick rounds at the men who'd taken to hiding behind a few overturned tables. One of the scarred man's partners leaned around to take a shot at Clint, but was cut down by the modified Colt before Clint's boots had touched the floor in front of the bar.

That gunman straightened up and dropped back as fresh blood soaked into the front of his shirt. He was dead before he even hit the floor.

Without stopping for so much as a second, Clint bent at the knees and rolled forward as he saw the other gunmen look up from where they'd been hiding. As he rolled toward the closest table, Clint heard shots explode around him. A few bullets punched through the floor to his right, which made it that much easier to decide which direction to fire at next.

Bringing himself to a stop in a one-knee stance, Clint shifted and fired at Jeff. He aimed specifically for a spot close to the first wound he'd given him. Sure enough, the scarred man let out a string of curses as hot lead ripped through the already bloody tear in his ribs.

Even though Jeff might have been tough enough to fight through the pain of that first wound, the second bullet was too much for him to bear. The scarred man turned white as a sheet and wobbled over like a poorly made stool.

"Clint!" Lyssa shouted as she stood up at the opposite end of the bar. "Duck!"

Seeing the gun pointed in his direction was more than enough cause for Clint to obey her command. The moment he dropped down, he heard the hiss of hot lead burning through the air over his head. That sound was followed by the slap of lead against flesh, soon to be followed by a pained grunt.

The other gunman that had accompanied Jeff into the saloon had somehow found a spot that Clint hadn't noticed. He'd still had his gun aimed at Clint when Lyssa's bullets found him. Now his arm drooped down and the gun slipped from his grasp as he staggered back and fell over.

Clint turned back to look at Lyssa and tipped his hat quickly. She had her eyes focused on where the scarred man had last been seen, but she did manage to give Clint a quick nod in return.

"Toss out your gun and we can put an end to this," Clint

said. Since he couldn't see exactly where Jeff had landed, he kept himself low and his Colt held at the ready.

"I wounded you on purpose," Clint warned. "That's so we could have a little talk. But don't think I'll wait for one moment if you don't give me a choice."

Looking over to Lyssa, Clint motioned for her to move around to one side of the overturned table while he got to the other. After another nod, she started circling in the proper direction.

"This might be a mistake," Clint said. "No need for any more blood to be spilled over it."

Since he didn't get a response, Clint gave Lyssa one more signal so they could both get around the table at the same time. When they got there, all they found was a bloody trail leading for the door.

SIX

With the smell of burnt gunpowder still fresh in his nose and
the blood pounding through his veins, Clint wasn't about to
stand there and wait while Jeff got away. He also wasn't
about to charge out through the front door without getting a
look out there first.

It seemed that Lyssa was thinking more of the first portion of that rather than the second, since she was already
headed for the door with her pistol in hand.

Clint ran up to her and took hold of her arm. "Hold up a
second," he said as she ripped her arm anxiously from his
grasp. After he saw that he had her attention, Clint pointed
to one side of the door while he stood on the other. Although
she wasn't too happy about it, Lyssa took the direction and
pressed her back to the wall next to the door.

Despite the way he presented himself, Clint wanted to
charge outside after Jeff just as much as Lyssa did. What
stopped him from doing just that was several years of experience in dealing with men who lived and breathed by the
guns in their hands.

Clint reached out with his free hand and pressed his palm
against the door. With a quick snap, he shoved the door open
and pulled his hand back inside. Just as he'd expected, a few

shots blazed through the air as someone outside shot at the first sign of movement.

Lyssa let out a breath and laughed under her breath. "Glad I followed your lead on that one."

"Me too. Now stay here and cover me."

"What are you going to—"

But before she could finish her question, Clint was through the door and hurrying outside. To her surprise, no more shots came from the street. Even so, she held her ground and prepared herself to shoot at anyone who stepped out of line.

Like everyone else inside the saloon, the folks on the street had ducked somewhere and weren't about to move. There were a few frightened whispers here and there, but nobody was foolish enough to so much as poke a head out from whatever cover could be found. Once she saw that the only gunmen inside the saloon were dead, Lyssa focused all her attention on what was happening outside.

Clint had been crouched behind a water trough and was now slowly standing up. He kept his Colt at the ready and his eyes fixed upon an alley across the street. The longer he waited without hearing so much as a peep coming from the street, the more tentative steps he took toward that alley.

Suddenly, a large shape filled the mouth of the alley as Jeff glared over the twin barrels of a sawed-off shotgun. Although he said something to Clint, his words were washed away by the roar of the shotgun as he pulled his triggers and filled the air with fiery smoke.

Clint could only grit his teeth and throw himself back down behind the trough as lead screamed straight toward him. Fortunately, the shotgun was loaded with buckshot rather than anything heavier. Because of that, the lead spread out good and wide before making it to Clint. He felt some of the buckshot rip his skin, but it wasn't anything more than a collection of scratches.

What concerned him more was the loud, familiar whinny that came from nearby.

Eclipse reared up on his hind legs and pumped his hooves in the air. Fresh blood trickled down the Darley Arabian's flank. When he dropped back down again, the stallion looked around with an angry glint in his eyes.

Knowing full well that Jeff had fired off both barrels and was a few seconds away from drawing his pistols again, Clint hopped over the water trough and charged straight toward the alley. Good to her word, Lyssa began firing from the saloon to keep Jeff pinned in right where he was.

"Son of a bitch!" Jeff grunted as he slung the shotgun over his back and felt the hot barrel press against his shoulder. He immediately grabbed one of his pistols, quickly replaced a few of the spent rounds and snapped the cylinder shut.

Since he hadn't used the street to get to the saloon, he knew the alley well enough to know where it led. In fact, that was the reason why he'd led his men in such a roundabout way in the first place. He didn't even think about leaving those other two behind. All that went through Jeff's mind was getting to where he needed to go while staying ahead of the people on his tail.

A few seconds later, Jeff could hear footsteps closing in behind him. Without breaking his stride, he shifted and fired a shot in the opposite direction.

Clint saw the man in front of him turn around. It was pure reflex that got him to grab onto the closest wall and flatten himself against it just as Jeff's trigger was pulled. The bullet whipped past him and Jeff kept moving.

"You're not getting out of here!" Clint shouted as he peeled himself from the wall and tore down the alley. "I can promise you that!"

"Aw, go to hell," Jeff replied.

Only a few more steps and Jeff would make it to the end of the alley. After that, it opened into a small lot where three horses were waiting. He knew that for certain because those horses belonged to him and his men. Jeff broke into a run and grabbed the first horse he could reach. It was a painful process, but he managed to pull himself up and into the saddle.

Clint could hear the sound of a horse and knew he could no longer afford to be cautious. With full knowledge of the risk he was taking, he lowered his head and ran as fast as he could to the end of that alley. Clint was ready to pull his trigger the moment he stepped into the open, but the only target he saw was a horse's ass.

Actually, he could also see the backside of the animal that the horse's ass was riding.

Out of sheer frustration, Clint straightened his arm and nearly pulled his trigger. He almost pulled it before thinking about all the wild shots that had already been taken. Rather than possibly shoot through someone's home by mistake, Clint lowered his gun and turned to run back through the alley.

SEVEN

Lyssa was about to head down that alley when she saw someone running out of it. She then almost fired a shot at the figure before recognizing Clint's face and letting out her breath. "Oh," she sighed. "It's you."

"Yeah, it's me. Who were you expecting?"

"I thought that maybe that asshole . . . Never mind. I'm glad you're safe. You are safe, aren't you?"

Clint patted himself down quickly as he stepped up to where Lyssa was waiting. "No holes in me. At least, none that weren't there before."

"What about that other one?"

"He got away."

"Got away? We can't just let him—"

"Don't worry," Clint interrupted as he examined Eclipse's flank. "We're not going to let him get anywhere."

Lyssa leaned forward and pulled in a quick breath when she saw the blood smeared over Eclipse's coat. "Oh my God. Is he all right?"

"Yeah. Looks like there's nothing too serious here. You can bet I'll be hearing about this for a while, though." Clint climbed into the saddle and had to hang on tightly as Eclipse immediately fussed and twitched at the sudden addition of weight to his back. "Oh, I'll be hearing about it for certain. There's no more bleeding, so he'll be fine."

"Where are you going?"

"After that fellow with the scars."

"Not alone, you're not," Lyssa said.

"You've got about three seconds. I'm not too wild on the notion of giving that shooter too much of a head start."

By the time Clint had finished saying that, Lyssa had already untied one of the horses from another post and climbed onto its back. It was a sandy mare with a light colored mane. She settled in and steered the horse toward the alley.

"Think you can track him as well as you did me?" Clint asked.

She nodded and replied, "No doubt about it."

"Good. Take off straight after him. He left a lot at the end of the alley and I think he was headed north. He's wounded, so I doubt he'll be up to traveling too far or too fast."

Although she looked anxious to get moving, Lyssa frowned a bit when she saw that Clint wasn't steering Eclipse in the same direction. "Aren't you coming?"

"I'm going to try and cut him off."

"Maybe I should come with you," she said warily.

Clint snapped his reins and leaned back to tell her, "Don't worry. If we're doing this right, we should meet up again when we catch up to that shooter. Besides, I've still got some things I need to ask you about before I give you the slip."

Even as he turned his back to Lyssa and headed around the corner, he could feel the tension building up beneath her skin. After taking so much pride in tracking him down, she didn't like being challenged with the possibility of him trying to get away. But there were more urgent matters to attend to at the moment, and if they didn't move quickly, those matters would leave both Lyssa and Clint in the dust.

It was a tight squeeze, but Lyssa's mare was able to fit down the alley. The lot at the other end was empty, but she spotted another narrow lane headed toward the north and rode down there. It didn't take much for her to see signs that someone had just ridden through there not long ago. If she strained her ears, she even picked up on the sounds of hooves pounding against the ground not too far in front of her.

Clint, on the other hand, wasn't so lucky.

He wasn't able to see any trace of Jeff or hear anything more than a few frightened voices as they shouted about what had happened at the saloon. As he rode, Clint plotted the quickest way for him to get in front of Jeff's horse. He might not have known that town inside and out, but he'd seen enough to figure out where he needed to be if he was to intercept someone trying to make a fast getaway.

As he bolted around a corner and sped up down the next street, Clint paid close attention to the way Eclipse moved and sounded while running. At first, the stallion was twitchy and irritable thanks to the fresh scrapes along his side. But the more he ran, the less he complained. Finally, Clint was fully convinced that the Darley Arabian hadn't been hurt much at all by that shotgun blast.

While that was fortunate for Eclipse, it was even more fortunate for the man who'd pulled that trigger.

Clint sped down the street, doing his best to weave around slower wagons and the occasional person trying to walk. He was also watching the buildings on his side, trying to figure where that lot at the end of the alley emptied out.

His best guess was a smaller street coming up quickly on his left. Clint pulled back on the reins, turned Eclipse toward that street and snapped them again. The stallion took the directions perfectly and made the turn like he was rounding a bend on a racetrack.

As Clint approached a small gap between two upcoming buildings, he smirked and drew his Colt. That gap was big enough to allow a horse to come through, and it was in the right spot for it to connect to that empty lot where he'd last seen Jeff.

Before he could get too optimistic, however, Clint saw another horse racing down the street and headed away from him. The dust in the air was still fresh enough behind that horse to show it had emerged from the very gap that he'd just spotted.

Clint slowed up so he could get a look down the narrow alley that connected to the street. Sure enough, it led to that lot, but there wasn't anything in there apart from more swirling dust. Shifting his eyes back to that other horse, he got Eclipse moving at full speed in its wake.

It was only a matter of seconds before that horse hit the end of the street, which then opened up onto empty land. Clint hunkered down and hung on for dear life as he coaxed Eclipse into a full gallop. The Darley Arabian seemed to have forgotten all about the gouges on his flank and was now committed to his stride.

The town rushed by Clint on both sides in a blur of wood planks and stacked bricks. Before long, he'd made it out of the town altogether and was able to see for miles in front of him. From this new vantage, it was easy to pick out the horse that he'd been chasing, since it was the only thing moving in plain sight.

Clint snapped the reins a few more times and saw he was catching up to the other horse with ease. It seemed that the only hard part was going to be getting Eclipse to slow down after such an explosive burst of speed.

Well before he pulled up alongside the other horse, Clint was able to make out the shape of the person riding it. All that accomplished was to confirm what he already knew: He'd just caught up with Lyssa.

"Where the hell did he go?" Clint asked.

Lyssa's first response was to turn and glare at Clint. Her gun was in her hand and she looked mad enough to use it even though she recognized Clint's face. "I was just about to ask that same thing. The bastard must have doubled back somewhere."

"Well he sure as hell isn't out here," Clint said while nodding toward the open expanse of trail ahead of them. "Let's circle back and ride the perimeter of town. I'll take the west side. You take the east."

She nodded and brought her horse around before digging her heels in and angrily snapping the reins. Clint and Eclipse had already disappeared within a cloud of dust.

EIGHT

Clint and Lyssa circled the entire town and even rode through it a few times before finally admitting defeat. By the time they met up again, the mess at the saloon was nearly cleaned up and folks were no longer afraid to show their faces outside again. They did seem more than a little nervous when they got a look at the two riders making their way back to the saloon where it had all started.

Ignoring the glances from various locals, Clint swung down from his saddle and stood on the boardwalk with his hands upon his hips. He was quiet for a little while, as if he expected to see Jeff or one of his men come riding by.

Lyssa dropped down from her own horse, but wasn't so quiet. "Damn! How the hell could he get away from me?"

"He outfoxed us," Clint replied grudgingly. "Plain and simple."

"Outfoxed us?"

"Well, he surely wasn't swept up by the hand of God. He's nowhere I can see, so that means he managed to get away from us without being caught. Sounds to me like a clear case of outfoxing someone."

She let out a breath and shook her head. "I guess you're right."

"But that doesn't mean we're done here."

"No?" she replied with a bit of hope in her eyes. "Did you see someone else who might know where to look?"

"Yeah. I'm looking right at her."

"Oh."

Clint took hold of Lyssa's elbow and pulled her away from the saloon. Lowering his voice while leaning forward, he said, "You mentioned a name a while ago."

"Sure I did. The name was Earp and I shouldn't have even said it so soon."

"Why not?"

"Because it was supposed to be a secret. At least, it was until we got further into California."

"Why the secrecy?" Clint asked. "Were you worried about someone hearing that name and taking a shot at us? Seems a bit late for that."

"You're right. Still, we should get riding since that asshole got away from us and all."

"Great. I'll lead the charge just as soon as I hear an explanation for all of this. Why would you be hired by someone like that just to bring me in? I know the Earps, so you'd best watch your step if you intend on lying to me about them or their intentions."

"I've got no reason to lie. The Earps have nothing to do with this asshole or those other gunmen with him today. In fact, I was sent to collect you before assholes like these ones here got wind that you were involved in this at all."

Clint felt his frustration growing inside of him like an ember. "I wasn't involved. Hell, I don't even know what this is and I'm already being shot at!"

"Now you see why it was supposed to be a secret." Lyssa looked around suspiciously at all the folks who were gathering around or peeking through nearby windows. "I was supposed to ask you for help on behalf of my employer and I was supposed to keep it quiet so you weren't put in too much danger should you refuse to come."

Clint had sat across from more than enough poker players

to spot a bluff when he saw one. Lyssa's face was definitely pretty, but it was also fairly easy to read. She wasn't bluffing. Even so, that didn't completely untie the knot in Clint's belly.

"That sounds fine," he said. "But I know for a fact you've been on my tail for days. And that's only as long as I've known you were there, so it might be even longer. If you wanted to find me and ask for my help, why go about it like that instead of just coming out and asking me?"

Lyssa looked at him as if it was all she could do to keep from shaking him. "Do you realize how hard it was for me to try and catch you?"

"Well, I—"

She cut in. "Hearing about you was easy enough. Hell, I heard that you were in so many places, I thought you'd sprouted wings just to get to them all. There were so many stories, rumors and speculations out there that sifting through them all was a goddamn nightmare!"

Clint reflexively took a step back as he saw the fire in Lyssa's eyes flare up even more.

But for every step Clint took back, she took one forward. It quickly seemed as though she was about to chase him all the way out of town.

"After Lord only knows how long, I finally managed to catch up to you," she continued. "And what happened? What did I get for all that trouble? Every time I got within a mile of you, you tore off like your ass was on fire. I started to believe that horse of yours really did have wings!

"Somehow, I managed to close the gap, but you still rode off without so much as a wave over your shoulder. For a man who I hear loves to help folks, you sure don't seem very good at talking to them."

Clint felt a chuckle building up in him, but knew better than to let it show. Of course, it wasn't as though Lyssa intended on giving him an opportunity to do more than let out a few stammering syllables.

"You say you caught me following you for a few days?"

she asked. "That's actually right about when I gave up trying to catch up to you and did everything but start shooting to get your attention. After all the work you put in to trying to shake me off your tail, you ask how come I didn't just walk up and ask you a simple question?"

Now that she was waiting for him to talk with her hands upon her hips, Clint figured he should say something.

"Well . . . it seemed reasonable to—"

Instantly, Clint knew he'd chosen the wrong thing to say.

"Reasonable?" she asked. "What part of that sounded reasonable to you?"

"I knew that there was plenty of people spreading talk and rumors about me. I guess I just didn't know that it could actually work in my favor."

Grumbling to herself, Lyssa climbed back into her saddle and flicked her reins.

Clint followed suit and was soon riding beside her. "Could you at least tell me what's so important that Wyatt Earp needs to track me down?"

"Wyatt Earp? Who said I was hired by Wyatt?"

NINE

The town was a small collection of shacks located less than a day's ride away from Colton, California. Although there wasn't much there, the few businesses that were clustered around that trickling little creek were fairly prosperous. The stores were supplied with fashions fresh off the boats from local harbors and got plenty of free advertising by word of mouth from the spoiled wives of rich men.

It was a little place that catered to a select group who considered going there a small excursion or even a vacation. The lawmen there were well armed, but rarely needed to arm themselves with more than harsh words simply because nobody but the rich shoppers even knew the town existed.

Those days were apparently over.

Xander Prouse rode in as quiet as any other visitor and sat as relaxed in his saddle as any other man who had money in his pocket and a pampered wife at home. Due to the dirt on his face and the gun at his side, Prouse got more than a few nervous glances tossed his way as he and Hobbes rode down the one and only street heading through town.

But, like true gentlemen, both riders merely smiled and tipped their hats before continuing along their way.

There weren't many people in town at the moment. For

the most part, there were just the couple of locals who owned and ran the businesses standing around and watching the wind blow on a slow day. Prouse and Hobbes stopped in front of the largest store, dismounted, and then strolled right into the place.

A bell over the door chirped merrily, alerting the shop-keeper of his two newest customers.

"Can I help you?" the man asked.

"Actually, I was looking for a nice set of cuff links," Prouse replied. "Maybe something in gold?"

The owner nodded and made his way over to a narrow glass case. "I know just the thing. Where you two from, anyhow?"

"Colton."

"Is that so? I know some folks in Colton."

"Yes. I'm sure that you do. I'll bet we know some of the same folks." The owner leaned down to unlock the case us-ing a key from his pocket, then slid back the panel and reached for a small, felt-covered tray holding cuff links as well as a few watches. "Who might that be?"

"A cocksucker by the name of Earp."

The owner's eyes snapped up at the sudden change in tone, and he found himself staring straight down the barrel of Hobbes's pistol. He froze in his spot, with his knees bent and his arms still halfway inside the display case. "What's the meaning of this?" the owner asked meekly.

"Shut up," Hobbes grunted.

Sidling up to the display case, wearing a broad grin, Prouse took a long look around, until he was convinced that there weren't any other customers in the store. "No need to get jumpy. Just call in your neighbors and be quick about it."

"Wh-what?"

"Your neighbors, your friends, anyone who might be around that you know of. Even the law, if you've got any of that around here."

Hobbes practically lit up when he heard that. "Yeah. Call in the law."

"I don't understand," the owner said.

"You don't need to. Just do it." Prouse's demand was punctuated by the metallic click of Hobbes thumbing back the hammer of his pistol.

"Jaime!" the owner shouted. "Get Randy and bring him in here!" When he saw the encouraging smiles on both gunmen's faces, he added, "And fetch all the deputies you can!"

There were a few affirming shouts, followed by the rattle of footsteps hurrying along the boardwalk outside.

"See?" Prouse said. "That wasn't so hard, was it?"

"Randy's a hell of a lawman," the owner said. "He won't tolerate whatever it is you're planning to do."

But neither of the gunmen responded to that. Instead, Prouse leaned forward and examined all the items in the case. "Oh. I think I'll change my mind. I'll take that silver watch right there instead of the cuff links."

What little hope that had been on the owner's face evaporated quicker than a drop of water upon a desert rock. A spark of that hope returned when the door to the shop opened and several men rushed inside.

"What the hell's going on in here?" roared a broad-shouldered man wearing a badge pinned to his shirt.

In a smooth motion, Prouse turned and aimed his pistol at the lawman. He pulled his trigger without speaking a word or even batting an eye and dropped the lawman with one shot through the head.

Hobbes took a second to drink in the look of panic on the owner's face before blasting that face with a single shot from his own gun. From there, he turned and added his own lead to the supply from Prouse to make short work of the deputies that had responded to the dead owner's call.

Of the two other deputies, one of them hadn't had the chance to get into the shop before the shooting started. For that reason alone, he was still standing and able to draw his weapon while his other two partners had already been cut down like wheat.

Windows shattered and wood splintered as more bullets

exploded from within the shop. The last deputy managed to squeeze off a few rounds, but those lodged harmlessly into the wall as he backpedaled away from the store. His heel knocked against the edge of the boardwalk, causing him to slip and tumble backward into the street. When his back slammed against the ground, he sent his last bullet into the air.

Prouse walked outside calmly with Hobbes behind him. Both men looked around at all the faces gaping at them from nearly every angle.

"Remember what you see here," Prouse declared. "Remember it especially when that piece of shit Earp comes by to check on his investment."

By now, Hobbes had already walked to stand directly over the surviving deputy. He took his time in pointing his gun at the deputy's forehead and then pulled his trigger.

TEN

Clint rode into Colton with Lyssa at his side. They'd made pretty good time since both of them were now in just as much of a hurry to get where they were going. Even so, Clint looked more than a little bit surprised.

"I honestly didn't think we'd get here until tomorrow," he said.

Lyssa smirked and said, "See how much easier it is to travel when one of us isn't running away from the other?"

"I hope I'll live that down sometime soon. Otherwise, I might just have to run away from you again."

"Don't do that. At least, not until we get to Main Street. Once I get paid, you can run off to wherever the hell you want."

"Aww, it's nice to see you so sentimental where I'm concerned."

"You're a nice fellow and all," Lyssa said, "but it seems like being around you is a whole lot more trouble that it's worth."

"Heh. You should try being me."

Although both of them shared a laugh, it seemed as though the entire ride was catching up to them at once. The road to Colton wasn't necessarily a tough one, but given the

39

way it had started, it had been an uneasy ride to say the least. Both Clint and Lyssa had spent a good portion of the time looking over their shoulders. The rest of the time had been spent looking in every other direction.

Without being able to let themselves relax for more than a minute or two at a stretch, even the few hours of sleep they'd gotten that night hadn't done much to loosen up the knots in their shoulders.

"Now that we're here," Lyssa mused, "I've got to admit this ride makes me feel pretty good."

"Have you been sipping from a flask without me catching you?"

"Nope. It's like my granddaddy used to say. Driving a rusty nail into your foot may not be the best thing in the world, but it sure feels good when you stop."

After the shoot-out with Jeff, the chase through the alleys, circling that town several times and the ride that followed it, Clint was just tired enough for that joke to make him laugh.

In fact, both of them were laughing as Lyssa brought her horse to a stop outside a modest storefront and climbed down from her saddle.

"This is the place, Clint," she said. "End of the trail. That is, unless you'd like to meet up a bit later."

"I'd like that."

For a moment, Clint and Lyssa just stood still and looked at each other. It wasn't so much of a sentimental thing as it was a quiet break between partners. Even though they'd only known each other for a day or two, they'd been through plenty in that amount of time.

Before another word could be said, the front door of the storefront swung open.

"Well, I'll be damned. If it ain't Clint Adams, himself."

The man who stood in the doorway was a tall fellow with thick hair and a bushy mustache, which covered a hearty portion of his face. Even though his cheeks were sunken a bit, the color of his face made him look both weathered and full of life.

A white shirt hung over a strong, solid frame. Somehow, even with his left arm supported by a sling, he still managed to look like he could knock out a horse with one punch. The gun and holster was so at home around his waist, that it was easy to miss. Then again, that might have been due to the bright smile that had taken residence under the man's graying mustache.

"Virgil," Clint said as he extended his hand. "It's been too long."

Even though Virgil Earp grabbed hold and shook Clint's hand, he only did so just long enough to pull him into a brotherly hug. After slapping Clint a few times on the back, he stepped inside and motioned for Clint and Lyssa to follow.

"I see you met the handiest tracker in California," Virgil said.

Lyssa beamed proudly and lowered herself into a chair against the wall.

"I did," Clint replied. "Although she could use a lesson or two in making a proper introduction."

"She is a bit rough around the edges, but she grows on you before too long."

The grin on Lyssa's face cooled off and she scowled at Virgil. "Watch yourself, old man."

Chuckling under his breath, Virgil walked over to a small desk and propped himself against it. The room was a sparsely furnished office with only a few mementos here and there to show that anyone actually used it more than a few days a month. Apart from a few chairs, the desk and a coat rack, there were only a couple pictures in worn-out frames as well as a couple newspapers preserved behind glass and hung on the wall.

"I hope your trip was fairly dull," Virgil said.

Hearing that, both Clint and Lyssa let out a wary chuckle.

Virgil's eyes narrowed and a severe expression came

onto his face like a black cloud passing over the sun. "What happened?"

"Nothing that a small posse couldn't have cured," Lyssa said.

"What's that supposed to mean? Clint, talk to me."

"There was a bit of trouble, Virgil," Clint replied. "But it wasn't anything we couldn't handle."

"I had a bit of trouble in Tombstone," Virgil said with a wry grin. "At the time, I thought I could handle it. Turned out it cost me plenty more than I figured." When he said that last part, Virgil's eyes drifted down to his left arm, which hung all but useless at his side.

"It wasn't anything that bad," Clint assured him. "At least, not yet. Eclipse took more lead than I did."

Virgil straightened up and looked as if he might charge like an angry bull. "You mean someone shot that Darley Arabian I heard about? Some son of a bitch is going to pay for that!"

"You can pay for a clean stall and some oats," Clint said. "That's all he needs. Before we worry about picking a stable, I'd like to hear about what was so important that I needed to be dragged all the way to Colton."

"Fair enough. Have a seat."

ELEVEN

The horse thundered along the trail so quickly that its hooves barely even seemed to touch the ground. Its head churned like a piston as foam began to form at the edges of its mouth. If it had been a little colder that day, steam would have been pouring from the animal's nostrils. As it was, the horse huffed and breathed like an engine struggling to roll up a mountainside.

The man in the saddle didn't appear to be in much better condition. His eyes were wide and set with grim determination upon the path ahead of him. His hands were closed in tight fists around the reins, snapping them every so often as if he thought his horse could go even faster.

Neither one of them slowed down until they bolted through Colton and came to a rough stop in front of a modest storefront where two other horses were waiting. The instant the man's boots hit the dirt, he was running for the front door. When he pushed it open, he looked straight past Clint and Lyssa to address Virgil Earp directly.

"There's been trouble, Marshal."

"Where?" Virgil asked as he straightened up.

"A trading post not far from here."

"How bad is it?"

43

Although the younger man was winded and flushed from his ride into town and his run into the office, he lost a good amount of the color in his face before saying, "Bad, Marshal. Real bad."

"Jesus Christ. I was hoping I'd have a bit more time."

"What's going on here?" Clint asked. "Is this why you wanted my help?"

"Partly. I can't say for certain just yet, but this may have something to do with a situation that's a bit too big for me to handle on my own. I've got a good bunch of boys working as deputies here, but they don't have the kind of experience we do."

"You want me to come along on this?" Clint asked.

Virgil took a deep breath as he slipped into his coat and double-checked his gun. "If you're seen with me too much, you might be pulled further into this mess whether you like it or not."

"So far, I don't even know what this mess is."

"And if you'd rather keep out of the line of fire, ignorance just might be bliss."

"Too late for that," Clint replied with a shrug. "No matter how ignorant I try to be, the lead still seems to fly around me."

Virgil grinned and nodded. "It sure as hell does. That doesn't mean I'm anxious to have any of that lead fly on my account."

"However I came to know that you were in trouble," Clint explained, "I still would have wanted to lend a hand."

"All right then. I figured I'd ask now since I won't have time to ask again later." Turning toward the deputy, Virgil nodded. "Let's head out."

The younger lawman practically bolted through the door, in much the same way he'd come in. Virgil was next outside and Clint followed him. After that, Lyssa brought up the rear. By the time she was outside, she spotted Virgil staring straight at her.

"Your part in this is done," Virgil said.

"I want to come along to—"

"No," Virgil said in a sharp tone that left no room for mis-understanding. "I've got my deputies and I've got Clint along with me. There's no need for anyone else."

"But I'd like to—"

"I said no. Don't make me say it again." With that, Virgil walked around the corner where his deputy was bringing his horse.

Clint pulled himself onto Eclipse's back and looked down at Lyssa. Even from that distance, he could see the anger brewing in her eyes as well as the twitch at the corner of her mouth. "Better stay put," he told her. "Virgil's in charge here."

"Yeah," she replied angrily. "I gathered that."

Leaning down a bit, Clint motioned for her to come closer. She did so grudgingly, but finally managed to get close enough for him to talk to her without being overheard by the rest of the lawmen.

"You want to help out?" he asked.

"That's what I said, isn't it?"

"Then check around town and see if you can dig up any talk about Virgil or anyone that might have it out for him."

Glaring up at him, she said, "You don't need to find work to keep me busy, Clint."

"That's not what I'm doing. I should get Virgil's side of the story soon enough, but I want to know if there's anything else going on. Since you like tracking things down, see if you can track down a line on that for me."

While she'd been reluctant or even angry at first, Lyssa now looked at Clint with less frustration in her eyes. "You seriously think I can find out something that nobody else can?"

"You found me, didn't you? A job like this should be easy."

"Doesn't pay as much, though."

"If you get something worth knowing, I'm sure you'll get enough of a fee to make it worth your while."

Although she nodded at that, it was plain to see that Lyssa wasn't necessarily worried about another payday.

"You coming or not?" Virgil growled in Clint's direction.

"I'm coming," Clint replied.

When Lyssa looked back at Virgil, she shot him another angry glare. "And I'm staying."

Virgil's response to that was a subtle nod before bringing his horse around and snapping the reins.

"Thanks," Clint said before pointing Eclipse in that same direction. "I really appreciate this."

"You'd better," she said. "Because I expect you to make good on my fee."

TWELVE

Clint knew that Eclipse could run like a bolt of lightning when called upon to do so. He also knew that other horses were pretty fast as well. But he would never have guessed that Virgil's old horse as well as the animals ridden by the deputies could move half as fast as they did when riding to that nearby trading post.

Eclipse had no trouble whatsoever in keeping up, but it seemed more like a race than simply trying to get from one spot to another. Then again, all of the Earps seemed to have that effect on folks. Apparently, that effect now carried over to horses.

"What are you grinning at?" Virgil asked as he looked over at Clint.

Shaking his head, Clint replied, "Nothing. Just wondering how come you haven't struck it rich as a jockey."

"This ol' gal has plenty of spark in her," he said while patting his horse's neck. "Just like the old boy riding her."

The grin on Virgil's face lasted another second or two before he spotted the small cluster of buildings straight ahead. "That's the place," he said. "Clint, I need you to ride around that side and see if you can find anyone lurking about. If

47

these are the same fellas I'm thinking of, they didn't just up and leave once they finished."

"You sure you don't need me as backup?"

"I've got deputies for that. Besides, you honestly may find plenty to keep you busy if you poke your nose under a few rocks."

Hearing that from anyone else, Clint might have thought he was being sent on a tedious job that was beneath a sworn-in deputy. But the look in Virgil's eyes was deadly serious, as was the tone in his voice. Besides, the Earps weren't known for beating around the bush. If Virgil said there were rats to be found, then Clint figured he'd better be ready for them.

Steering off the path, Clint veered away from the lawmen so he could circle around the back of the buildings Virgil had shown him. Already, he could see plenty of folks emerging from the buildings and gathering at a spot directly in Virgil's path. Since they were anxious to greet the older lawman, they didn't pay much mind to where Clint was going.

"Over here, Marshal!" one of the men said while waving frantically.

Virgil slowed up a bit and came to a stop in front of the first building. After swinging down from his saddle, he took a careful look around using eyes that glinted like a hawk's. "What happened here?" he asked once he'd taken in his surroundings.

"They killed Mr. Hardigan!"

"Who did?"

"Some men rode in and killed him! Barely even stole much of anything from the place. They just killed them all and rode away."

"Killed them all?" Virgil asked. ""Who got hurt? Tell me everything."

The man was in his early forties and had a large belly hanging over his belt. Sweat glistened upon his face and neck as though the act of talking was just as strenuous as running a mile uphill. "They shot Mr. Hardigan and then killed the sheriff as well."

"Mead's dead?"

The fat man nodded. "Him and both his deputies."

Virgil's only reaction was for his expression to turn to stone as he stared at the spot that everyone else seemed to be avoiding. "Is that them over there?" he asked gravely.

Taking a quick look for himself, the fat man nodded again. "We left them there until someone could take them away. We're waiting for an undertaker from Colton."

But Virgil had already started walking to the store. His jaw was set into a firm line and his right hand rested upon the grip of his pistol. He had no trouble spotting the bodies laying on the boardwalk and walked right up to them. He looked at each dead face in turn before stepping into the store.

A few seconds later, Virgil emerged and carefully studied every one of the folks gathered in the street. "Did anyone see or hear what happened?"

When he saw nothing but frightened eyes staring back at him, Virgil added, "I came here to track down these animals and bring them to justice. Anyone who wants to help can do it now or keep quiet and listen to their guilty consciences every night hereafter. I swear to you, whoever did this will be too busy running to worry about figuring out who told anything to me."

There were a few volunteers who stepped forward. Once they started talking and Virgil took in every word they said, those volunteers were joined by even more. Soon, the marshal and his deputies were overrun with folks willing to give their account of the slaughter.

THIRTEEN

Clint left Eclipse nearby so he could move around behind the buildings on foot. Now that he'd seen the crowd Virgil had attracted, he saw the reasoning behind wanting someone to sneak around behind them all to get a look from another angle.

From where he was standing, Clint could see a few scattered men standing near the crowd just so they could watch it. More importantly, they seemed to be keeping close tabs on the lawmen themselves. Out of those few people, one or two of them were watching a little too closely to be doing so out of casual interest.

Clint studied their faces as best he could and then moved on to see about getting a closer look. There were plenty of reasons why someone might want to watch over the law in a situation like this. It might be the same morbid curiosity that forced them to look into the eyes of a dead body. It might be nothing more than boredom.

Then again, it might be survival.

The best way for killers to prosper was to keep the law in sight without letting them get too close. A smart killer would have figured this out for himself. A professional killer would have had the practice down to a science.

As Clint walked behind the stores, he got closer and closer to the one that was actually at the middle of this storm. The smell of burnt gunpowder and blood was still in the air, so Clint did his best to focus on his other senses. Somehow, no matter how hard he tried to divert his attention, the stench of death would not be ignored.

Clint was still trying to focus on everything but his nose when his ears picked up on something. Under normal circumstances, the little peep he heard might have been washed away amid the numerous other voices that were swirling in the air.

At this time, however, Clint not only heard this peep, but he also had a pretty good guess as to where it had come from.

Looking down, Clint's eyes darted along the bottom of the more narrow boardwalk that connected the backs of the stores in the row. He quickly spotted a rut in the dirt beneath the boards, which was only slightly shallower than a ditch. Still, it was deep enough and wide enough to allow a small figure to crawl beneath the boardwalk and watch it from hiding.

Clint could see another set of eyes looking back at him from those dusty shadows. After holding that gaze for more than a second, however, he saw the little face under there start to wriggle out of sight.

Slowly, Clint knelt down and clasped his hands together. He made sure the Colt was out of sight and mostly hidden by his arm as he stared into the space beneath the boardwalk.

"Come on out of there," Clint said softly. "Nobody's going to hurt you."

For a moment, Clint thought that the face he'd seen under there was already long gone. As much as he wanted to try and find it again, he knew better than to try and outfox someone who probably knew the space beneath those boards like the back of their hand. Fortunately for him, Clint spotted that face once more as it reluctantly came into view.

"There you are," he said. "Why don't you come out of there?"

The voice that drifted out was only slightly louder than a mouse's squeak. "I can't."

"Don't be scared."

"I'm not scared. I'm . . . stuck."

Trying not to laugh at the urgency within that little voice, Clint scooted forward and slowly reached out with both hands. "You want me to help you out of there?"

"Are those bad men around?"

"It's just me out here and I'm with the law."

The little eyes peering out from under the boardwalk suddenly grew wide. "You're with Marshal Earp?"

"I sure am."

That was enough to coax a set of little hands from under the boards. Clint took hold of them and pulled. Attached to those hands were skinny arms, a narrow body and a face framed with light brown hair. Before a set of legs could be seen, the child was snagged upon something and refused to come out any further.

"See?" the little girl said. "I told you I was stuck."

Clint hunkered down a bit more and reached his hand under the boards. Before too long, he felt where the girl's dress had caught upon a nail. In fact, the nail was snagged through a few skirts as well as her belt, keeping her from coming out any further. It took a little cautious work, but Clint finally managed to free her from the nail.

"There you go," Clint said as he pulled his arm out. "Let's give this another shot."

This time, when he pulled her arms, Clint felt the girl slide out without a hitch. She jumped to her feet and brushed off the first few layers of dirt that covered her dress.

"Thank you, mister," she said.

"What's your name?"

"Molly."

"What were you doing under there, Molly?" Clint asked.

"Hiding from the bad men."

"What bad men?"

"I saw them ride up to Mr. Hardigan's store and they scared me so I ran away."

"Did any of them try to hurt you?"

Molly shook her head. "No, but they were bad men. My ma told me how to spot bad men and she said to run if I ever saw one."

"Your ma sounds like a smart lady," Clint said, which put a bright smile on Molly's face. "How long were you under there?"

"I don't know."

"Did you hear any shooting?"

She nodded. "I heard the bad men talking to Mr. Hardigan."

Clint did his best to seem more concerned than eager, so as not to get Molly any more nervous than she already was. "Really? Can you tell me what they said?"

Scrunching her face as she thought it over, she tapped her chin while pondering the question. The girl couldn't have been more than six years old, but she spoke more deliberately than plenty of adults Clint had met. Only after she was good and ready did Molly answer Clint's question.

"They said they wanted to send something," she told him.

"Send something?" Clint asked. "Like a letter or such?"

"No. A message."

"They wanted to send a message?"

She nodded.

"Send a message to who?"

Even though Molly seemed anxious to answer, she bit her tongue and shut her lips tightly. Finally, she whispered, "I'm not supposed to say words like that."

"Did the men say bad words?" Clint asked.

She nodded.

"I'm sure it would be all right this one time. I mean, you're just telling what someone else said. It would be a great help, you know." When he saw that he wasn't getting too far with that particular argument, Clint decided to pull out the big gun. "I bet even Marshal Earp would appreciate it if you helped out by telling what you heard."

That pushed Molly almost to the point where she seemed ready to bust. Leaning on one foot so she could see the group gathered around the famous lawman, she let out her words along with a gasping breath. "He said he had a message for that cocksucker Earp." Those words must have sounded worse out loud than they did in her mind because Molly quickly slapped both hands over her mouth and kept them there.

Clint made sure the expression on his face didn't even begin to change. "It's all right. What else did they say?"

"There was a bunch of shooting and after that, one of the men said he knew Marshal Earp would come running and when he did, he could deliver a message he would never forget."

Those words hit Clint like an axe handle right between the eyes. The implication behind them got his heart pounding and his blood racing through his veins.

"What happened after you heard that?" he asked. Even though he tried not to alarm the girl, he wasn't able to keep as calm as he had a few moments ago. "It's real important. What happened after that?"

"Ummm . . ."

Clint fought back the urge to ask her again. The little girl was obviously starting to inch away from him and toward the relative comfort of the space beneath the boardwalk.

"They didn't say anything after that," she told him.

"Are you sure?"

"Yessir. They might have, but I couldn't hear it since I was under the floor. I heard them shoot some more and then they walked out. After that, I heard horses."

"Horses? You mean you heard horses coming or going?"

"They were going. The horses ran off and I didn't hear the men anymore after that. I wanted to find my ma, but I got stuck."

"You did real good, Molly," he said quickly as he

scooped her up into his arms. "I'm going to take you over to talk to the marshal."

Molly was so happy that she barely even noticed she was being tucked under Clint's arm like a rolled-up newspaper. She smiled right up to the point where she was turned right-side-up and set upon her feet less than an arm's length away from Virgil Earp himself.

"This is Molly," Clint said. "She heard something she'd like to tell you about."

Virgil looked down at the girl with confusion etched across his face. "Where'd you find this little sugarplum?" he asked in a way that made his gruff voice sound vaguely sweet.

"She'll tell you the story. I'm headed back to Colton."

"What? Why?"

"Just give me a head start so I can get back to town without everyone noticing. There might be some trouble brewing."

"I'm coming with you," Virgil insisted.

"No, you're not. Things like this are what you wanted me around for, remember?"

Virgil obviously wasn't accustomed to taking orders. That notwithstanding, he slowly nodded and turned his back to Clint. He was unable to maintain the stern frown on his face when he saw that Molly was still gazing up at him adoringly.

FOURTEEN

Even if there might have been a few eyes and ears left behind by the killers, Clint knew that the men behind those deaths were nowhere in the vicinity. Whatever business they had with Virgil, they didn't have the guts to face him just then. If they had, they wouldn't have had any problem finding him. Clint knew better than anyone the lengths someone would go to to set up someone rather than face him head-on.

They seemed to be delivering a message. Molly's words went hand in hand with the bodies strewn throughout that trading post to prove that much. And if they wanted to deliver an even more powerful message, the best place to do that was in Colton.

Being the cowards they were, it made perfect sense for the killers to wait until Virgil thundered out of Colton so they could slide in and write their message in blood. Too bad Clint hadn't had enough information to put all of that together until it might be too late.

Eclipse covered the distance between the trading post and Colton in record time. Perhaps the Darley Arabian picked up on Clint's own excitement, but he seemed ready to run back and forth a few more times even after making it back to Colton.

"You can rest for a bit now, boy," Clint said as he gave Eclipse a pat while jumping down from the saddle. He lashed the reins around a nearby post and rushed along the rest of the side streets on foot.

Clint might not have known exactly what he was looking for and he might not have known exactly where to look, but he doubted he'd have to search too hard to find it. Sure enough, he got a real good indication of where to go when he heard a shot fired less than two streets away.

Another shot followed soon after it, causing Clint to draw his Colt before he got a look at any specific target. He knew he wouldn't have to wait long, however, since there was a commotion headed straight for him from across the next street. What surprised him the most was who was flushing that commotion in Clint's direction.

"Hey!" Lyssa shouted as she bolted through a doorway with a gun in her hand. "Come back here!"

The man she'd been shouting at didn't so much as glance over his shoulder. He was too busy shoving through a small group of men who'd been on their way into the building where Lyssa was standing.

It was after dark, so Clint pressed himself against the closest building and dropped his Colt back into its holster so as not to draw any suspicion from the approaching runner.

Clint narrowed his eyes as if that might help him blend in a bit more within the shadows. By keeping perfectly still, he was able to study the approaching man that much closer. He wasn't a big fellow and his face didn't ring any bells inside Clint's mind. He was carrying a gun, however, which told Clint more than enough.

"I'm not through with you," Lyssa shouted at the man's back. Judging by the way she stayed in the doorway rather than chase the guy, she'd either lost him in the small crowd outside or her eyes hadn't adjusted to the darkness.

"You're through all right, you crazy bitch," the man grumbled under his breath as he slowed to a quick walk. "And you ain't the only one."

When Clint stepped forward, he appeared to the other man like a ghost that had peeled out of the shadows clinging to a wall. It was such a shock that the man gasped and nearly fell over his own feet trying to step away from him.

"What was that supposed to mean?" Clint asked, taking full advantage of the fright he'd put into the other man.

"Wh-what?"

"You just said she was through. What did you mean by that?"

Although the other man might have been scared at first, that shock had already worn off by the time Clint took a few more steps. Gritting his teeth, he balled up his fists and took a swing at Clint's jaw.

Clint leaned back just far enough to avoid the punch and then lashed out with one of his own. It wasn't the hardest punch he could manage, but it connected with enough force to stun the guy for a second or two. By the time the man shook it off, Clint was practically on top of him.

"I just came from that trading post," Clint rasped. "You left plenty of bodies outside that general store."

"That wasn't me," the man stammered. "It was them others. I'm just a scout."

"Scouting for who?"

The man snarled like a cornered weasel and made a quick grab for Clint's throat. Even though he managed to get his hands around Clint's neck, he only managed a twitching squeeze before Clint brought both arms up within the man's grasp and knocked his hands away to either side.

"I asked you a question, asshole," Clint said. "Who asked you to do this scouting?"

The man's arms moved as if they were on well-oiled hinges. Before Clint could get ahold of him, the man reached around to grab a knife that hung at his belt, just beneath his jacket. The blade came out and up to swipe at Clint's chest.

Although Clint managed to step back to avoid any serious injury, he still felt the scrape of steel against his skin. The knife was sharp as a razor and sliced through his shirt without a problem. When he felt the sting of the fresh cut, Clint put a little extra muscle into his punch and slammed his fist into the man's gut.

"You know what I'm talking about," Clint said as he grabbed hold of the man's shirt and pulled him in closer. Lifting his knee while pulling the man into him, Clint doubled the guy over and drove all the air from his lungs.

Now that he could barely breathe, the guy could no longer hold onto his knife and let it drop through his fingers. Clint kicked it away with the sweep of one foot and slammed his knee into the man once more for good measure.

"Doesn't matter if you talk to me right now or not," Clint told him. "There's a jail cell close by where you can collect your thoughts."

Just then, Lyssa ran up to them with her gun drawn and a surprised look on her face. "Clint? When did you get back?"

FIFTEEN

The door to the jail cell slammed shut with a jarring rattle. The only sound to make the man inside shudder more was the clanging of the key being turned in the lock. After that, the man Clint had captured wandered to the back of the cell and flopped down onto the rickety old cot provided by the township of Colton.

Clint stood next to the deputy who had the keys and grinned through the bars at the prisoner.

"When did you say Marshal Earp would be back?" the deputy asked.

"Shouldn't be too long. Less than another few hours, I'd say."

"It's already pretty dark."

"That won't matter to Virgil."

The deputy only had to think about that for a second before he chuckled and nodded. "Yeah, you're right about that. Where are you going?"

"I was going to see about finding a room for the night. Any suggestions?"

"Well," the deputy muttered while shifting on his feet. "Since the others aren't back yet, I was actually hoping

61

you'd stay here for a while. You know, just in case that one's friends come along."

Clint took a good look at the deputy. He was a younger man and didn't have the impetuous spark in his eyes that plagued most men his age. While he might have been a bit overcautious, the deputy also wasn't eager to use his gun or storm out to solve the town's problems on his own. All in all, those were very good traits to have in a deputy.

"We're spread pretty thin with Marshal Earp out of town and the rest of us smoothing out that fight in the Rusty Nail."

Although that name wasn't immediately familiar to Clint, he recalled seeing a sign over the door both Lyssa and the man in the cell had come through earlier that night.

"Besides," the deputy continued with the hint of authority in his voice, "the marshal said you were here to lend a hand."

"I know you're doing your job, but I don't think the rest of this one's friends will be showing their faces for a little while. In fact, I'd say right about now is one of the few quiet times we'll have for a bit."

"How can you be so sure?"

"Because this one's a scout," Clint explained. "And scouts are sent ahead before the rest come marching in. It'll take a while for the others to know this one's gone."

"How do you know he's a scout?"

"Because he told me so."

The deputy chuckled and looked back and forth between Clint and the man in the cage as if waiting for the punch line of a joke. When the line didn't come, he said, "Assholes like this lie all the time."

Clint stared directly at the man in the cell until the prisoner turned away and put his back to the bars just to escape the burning glare. With a satisfied grin, Clint said, "He's too scared to lie."

All it took was a couple seconds of studying the prisoner cowering in his cell for the deputy to get the same grin that Clint was wearing. "I guess you're right about that," he said

in a voice that was more natural than when he'd been trying
to put his foot down. "Marshal Earp said you knew your way
around killers. He even said you were there in Tombstone."

Hearing the name of that town brought a flood of memories into Clint's mind. For a second, he thought he could feel
the harsh Arizona wind blowing sand and gunsmoke into his
face. "I was there," Clint said in a tone that was meant to dis-
courage any more questions. "Now do you have a hotel you
can recommend?"

"Sure," the deputy said with a quick nod. "Try the Pacifica a few blocks down."

"Thanks." Clint started to leave, but stopped short before
exiting the room. He turned around and said, "I didn't catch
your name."

"It's Cole."

"Good working with you, Cole. When Virgil gets back,
tell him I'll check in here in the morning."

"Will do."

With that, Cole pulled up a stool and sat at a small table
in the corner of the room. He picked up a newspaper and got
to reading while the prisoner acted like he was sleeping on
his cot.

Clint stepped out of the jail and took a deep breath of
fresh air. He didn't even have a chance to let that breath out
before Lyssa walked up to him with her hands stuck in her
pockets.

"I was going to get that guy myself, you know," she said.

Clint nodded. "Yeah, you chased him right out to me. Was
he the only one?"

"So far."

"That's what I thought." Clint then walked up to her and
slid his arm around her waist so he could pull her right along
with him as he kept moving.

Although she seemed a little surprised to be swept up like
that, she didn't fight it. "Don't you want to hear about what
happened?" she asked.

"Later."

"Did you at least hear the lowdown from Marshal Earp on what's been going on?"

"We were too busy tearing up the trail between here and some trading post. I'm sure I'll hear about it tomorrow."

"You don't seem too concerned."

"No matter how good or bad things are, they'll still be here in the morning. Right now, I'd just like to find the Pacifica Hotel and get a room. Can you help me out?"

"I can help you, but the first thing to do is avoid the Pacifica. That place is dirty and the service is terrible. I won't even mention the food."

"That's the place the deputy recommended."

"Which is probably why the owners of the Pacifica are so damn lazy. Come to the Prospector. It's this way," she said while steering him down another street. "Their beds are softer, plus there's other comforts."

"Like what?"

"Like me."

SIXTEEN

Clint didn't even bother stopping at the front desk. Instead, he allowed himself to be led by the hand up the stairs and into Lyssa's room. Along the way, they did get a stern look from a short man wearing spectacles who was sweeping the front room.

"This is a respectable place," he said to Clint and Lyssa's backs. "Unless you two are married, I'll have to insist that—"

"Don't worry about it," Lyssa said with an offhanded wave. "I'm just collecting on a debt."

They didn't know if that pacified the clerk or not, since both Clint and Lyssa were inside her room before the bespectacled man could answer.

It was a small but comfortable room lit by a single lantern burning as low as it could without going out. The dim glow of the lantern was barely enough to allow them to get across the room without tripping over anything.

After kicking the door shut with his heel, Clint asked, "What's this debt you're talking about?"

"You said we'd have some time together, remember?"

"I thought it was dinner."

Lyssa slid her hand along Clint's stomach and then

worked her way until she was feeling between his legs. "You want to argue, or would you rather have your way with me?"

After making a show of thinking that over, Clint took hold of her shirt and pulled it straight over her head. Since the clothing was baggy on her, it came off without a hitch, leaving Lyssa standing there wearing nothing but her jeans, boots, a camisole and a shocked smile.

"I've had enough arguing for a while," Clint said.

The camisole was made of thin cotton and was the tightest piece of clothing she wore. Compared to the bulky shirts and jackets which were cut more for a man's body, the undergarment was more than a pleasant surprise. It hugged the curves of her breasts like a second skin, and the dim light from the lantern accented her erect nipples.

Lyssa lowered her head and gave Clint a seductive smile. She took hold of his shirt gently and then ripped it open in one strong motion. She laughed a bit when she saw how she'd managed to put a shocked grin on Clint's face for a change.

"You talk a lot," she said while unbuckling her jeans and peeling them down over her hips. "I've been thinking of a new way for you to use that mouth of yours." With that, she kicked off her boots and jeans and then sat down on the edge of the bed.

It seemed the camisole wasn't the only feminine piece of clothing she wore. Beneath her jeans was a set of short silk underpants that wrapped around her hips like icing that had been drizzled onto a cake. She kept her eyes on Clint while slowly spreading her legs.

Clint stepped forward and placed his hands upon her knees. When he looked down to her smooth curves and soft skin, he could see the moisture between her legs already soaking into the underpants she wore. He got down to his knees and removed her panties so he could get a good look at the soft pussy wrapped within them.

The moment his fingers drifted across the lips of her vagina, Clint could feel Lyssa's body trembling. When he leaned forward to kiss her, she tensed in anticipation before letting out a breath when she felt his lips upon her inner thigh.

Lyssa leaned back upon one elbow and reached out with her other hand to play with Clint's hair. She propped one leg on the edge of the mattress and moved her hips forward as Clint's mouth drifted closer to where she wanted it to go.

Deciding he'd tortured her long enough, Clint used his tongue on her most sensitive spots while reaching up to cup her breasts in both hands. Lyssa immediately let out a long gasp and grabbed hold of the back of Clint's head. Her hips twitched and pumped against his face slightly as Clint's tongue worked its magic between her legs.

It didn't take long before her entire body was trembling and she was gasping in quick, short bursts. When her climax approached, Lyssa forced her eyes open so she could get a look at what Clint was doing. When she saw him looking right back at her, she was pushed over the edge and into a powerful orgasm.

By the time she opened her eyes again, Clint was settling on top of her. She hadn't even realized that she'd dropped back to lay flat upon the bed. Rather than try to recall when she'd laid down, she reached up and clasped her hands behind Clint's neck and opened her legs for him.

Her body was taut and smooth at the same time. Tight muscles resided beneath soft flesh, giving Clint's entire body a treat as he laid on top of her. He could feel her legs wrap tightly around him, and once he slipped his penis into her, he could feel those muscles tightening as well.

Slowly, Clint eased inside of her. The more of his cock she took into her, the wider Lyssa smiled. Clint let out a slow breath until he'd buried himself completely within her moist embrace. Lyssa's grip around him loosened just a bit as she laid back to savor the feel of him moving in and out of her.

Clint pumped back and forth, working his cock within her until he was even harder than when he'd started. At that point, his instinct took over and his thrusts became more powerful and his arms wrapped tightly around her.

Lyssa leaned back and stretched out her arms like a cat lounging on a blanket. When she felt her fingers brush against the headboard, she stretched out a bit more until she could grab hold of a post.

Clint felt her moving beneath him and straightened up so he was kneeling on the mattress between her open legs. Reaching underneath her, he lifted her up just enough so he could scoot her back a few inches, and she immediately grabbed the headboard with her other hand.

Looking down at her, Clint took a moment to admire the lines of her body as she stretched out upon the mattress. Her nipples were fully erect and stood up proudly upon her breasts. They got just a bit harder as he rubbed them with both hands and let his palms drift over the sensitive skin. With one hand, Clint lifted Lyssa's leg up off the bed. With his other hand, he guided himself back inside of her and thrust his hips forward.

Clenching her eyes shut, Lyssa let out a soft moan as she was filled up by Clint's stiff cock. She took his direction willingly and rested her leg on his shoulder. That way, she was spread open even more to accommodate him as he pumped in and out of her.

As much as he wanted to keep his hands upon her breasts, Clint couldn't help but slide his hands under her so he could cup her tight buttocks. The distraction was more than worth it since he was then able to lift her backside off the bed and draw her closer to him as he thrust powerfully between her legs.

"Oh my God," she exclaimed as her eyes shot open. Before those words were even completely out of her mouth, another orgasm was working its way through her body. It arrived fully after Clint pumped a few more times. By then, she was thrusting her hips forward in time to his rhythm and grinding against him to prolong her pleasure.

Without letting go of her backside, Clint buried his cock in her again and again. The feel of her wet lips wrapped around him combined with the feel of her tight ass in his hands would have been more than enough to send him into a climax. Listening to her moan and call out his name gave him an orgasm that knocked the wind right out of him.

When Clint fell onto the bed in exhaustion, he and Lyssa were breathing as if they'd run all the way across the state and back. That's when they heard a tapping on the door and a meek voice coming from the other side.

"Excuse me," the clerk squeaked through the door. "What's going on in there?"

Clint and Lyssa had just enough strength to laugh.

SEVENTEEN

Xander Prouse rode into Colton as the sun was just beginning to make its presence known in the sky. He didn't have his head held as high as he had when he'd ridden into the last few towns, but that was all part of his plan.

He'd figured on sneaking into town without being noticed, but that didn't account for the scowl on his face. That was there because of what he hadn't heard that he'd been expecting for the better part of the previous night.

Hobbes rode beside him, wearing a scowl that didn't look much different from the one he usually wore. "We probably just missed him somewhere along the way," he grumbled.

For a moment, it didn't seem that Prouse would even acknowledge that with a response. When he did, it came in the form of taut words forced through a clenched throat. "Bill ain't stupid enough to miss us along the way. He got found out, caught or killed along the way. That's what happened."

"Which do you think it is?"

"I don't bother guessing about things like that," Prouse said. "I'd rather know for certain. That's where you and the rest of these men come into it."

Hobbes nodded grimly. "I'll do whatever it takes. You know that."

"I know, Hobbes. This time, I don't want you getting shot up again. This requires a steadier hand and a touch of discretion. For that, I want you to send someone else in who can see what happened to our scout."

"If he got killed or caught, that shouldn't be too hard to find out. Folks usually like talking about something like that."

Prouse nodded and quickly added, "That's the easy part. Since we've lost Bill for the moment, I need someone to finish up the job he was sent to do. That's where the discretion comes in."

Hobbes glanced over his shoulder and studied the faces of the men trailing behind them. Since the group didn't want to ride into town like an invading army, they were scattered along the street, and a few were even out of sight completely. Finally, Hobbes nodded to himself and turned back around.

"Jarrett should do nicely," Hobbes said.

"Fine. See to it and check back in with me later. We'll meet up at that spot we picked outside of town."

"When?"

"An hour after sundown. That should give us enough time to get a feel for this place and see what happened to Bill. And if you need to take extra time in getting out there, do it. This ain't a raid like the last bunch of towns we've been through. This is the real show."

But Hobbes was already pulling back on his reins and signaling to some of the other men. "I know, I know. This is the whole reason we're out in this neck of the country."

"You can say that again. We've got one more message to send, and when it's delivered, we're gonna be more famous than those fucking Earps ever were."

EIGHTEEN

Virgil stepped out of a small restaurant across the street from the Pacifica Hotel. He wiped the ends of his mustache with the back of his hand and stood outside while content- edly patting his belly. At the sound of approaching foot- steps, he turned and started to step aside. When he saw that Clint was the one approaching, Virgil blinked a few times in surprise.

"What's the matter, Virgil?" Clint asked with a laugh. "Did you think I'd ride off and never be seen again?"

"No. I just thought you were staying at the Pacifica. I spent my whole breakfast watching the place through the restaurant's window."

"I don't know if that should make me nervous or not, but I do apologize for the mix-up. I got another recommendation after I last talked to your deputy."

"That's quite all right. He only steers folks to the Pacifica because I'm part owner of the place."

"Still a businessman, huh?"

"Well, that's the only way a man can prosper nowadays. Wearing a badge might be fun and all, but it doesn't put as much food on the table as running a business."

"Fun?" Clint asked. "Is that what you call it?"

"Sometimes. Hell, I don't know. It beats saying that I don't know any better."

Clint walked into the restaurant and saw it was about half-full. He went to the table at the back of the room and sat so he could watch the door. Without even thinking about it, Virgil took the second chair and situated it so he could watch the door as well.

"How's Wyatt?" Clint asked after he sat down and ordered a pot of coffee.

"Wyatt's Wyatt. Sometimes that's all that needs to be said on that subject."

"Sounds like he's doing about the same then."

"You might have seen him more recently than I have."

"Doesn't he come around to visit? I know Wyatt was always the sort to keep his family close."

"Used to be," Virgil said as a shadow seemed to fall across his face. "Now he's just trying to put some men in their graves in the name of family. Ever since Tombstone, it's been hard to talk any sense into that boy."

Virgil Earp was the only man Clint had ever met who could call Wyatt Earp "boy" and get away with it. Anyone else could barely get something like that out of his mouth without shuddering or looking over his shoulder. It didn't even matter if Wyatt wasn't anywhere in sight.

Clint had seen Wyatt change after the dustup in Tombstone between his family, Doc Holliday, the Clantons and McLowerys. To say it wasn't pretty was a gross understatement. Truth be told, for anyone who wasn't there for the whole mess, there weren't many words that could describe it.

After the smoke had cleared, the factions were still taking shots at one another until Virgil sustained the shotgun wound that nearly crippled him, Morgan Earp was killed and Wyatt took off to avenge him.

"You hear about what that boy's been doing?" Virgil asked.

"Bits and pieces. I've heard that he's been going after the

men that shot you and Morgan. Anyone who knows Wyatt wouldn't have any trouble believing that."

Virgil nodded solemnly and spoke in a dark tone. "He's caught up to a few of them."

"Really? I hadn't heard anything for certain. What happened?"

After taking a quick look to see that no one was close enough to hear him when he lowered his voice, Virgil grumbled, "Let's just say the men Wyatt found won't be standing trial."

Coming from a pure-blooded lawman like Virgil Earp, those words didn't reflect too well upon his brother. "And that doesn't leave this room, you understand?" The way he fixed his glare upon Clint was an unspoken request to keep that information among themselves.

Actually, it was more of an unspoken threat.

In the silence that followed, the coffee was brought to their table by a smiling woman wearing a blue and white checked dress.

"Another breakfast for you, Marshal?" she asked cheerily.

"Just coffee," Virgil replied briskly.

Shifting her eyes quickly away from Virgil, the woman took Clint's food order and left the table.

Even though he knew how much Virgil wanted to put the subject to rest, Clint couldn't let it lie. "So," he said cautiously. "Wyatt's gone hunting, then?"

Even though he was frustrated by the conversation, Virgil knew it would take more than a few stern words to get Clint to drop anything. "If that's what you call it."

"Look, I don't want to poke a hornet's nest, but Wyatt's my friend too. I don't need to know every last thing, but it would be nice to know if he's taking care of himself."

Virgil let out a sigh and sipped his coffee. "Last I heard, he was still healthy." Suddenly, a smile cracked his face and he shook his head like the concerned older brother he was. "Although, how he manages that with the life he leads is anyone's guess."

"Like you said, Wyatt's Wyatt."

"Speaking of old friends, have you heard anything about Doc?"

"It's been a while," Clint replied. "You're talking about Doc Holliday, right?"

Virgil shrugged and said, "Yes, that's the one."

"I always figured you preferred not hearing about him."

"Doc's not my favorite person, but he stuck by all of us when the chips were down."

"I caught up with him in Leadville a while back," Clint said. "He didn't look so good."

"That's a shame."

"Since we're catching up on old times, how about you fill me in on why I was brought here? I'd also like to know who's been shooting at us."

NINETEEN

After pulling in a slow breath, Virgil still didn't seem comfortable with what he was about to say. So, instead of trying to figure out a better set of words to use, he just spat out the first ones that came to mind.

"Have you ever heard of a man by the name of Xander Prouse?"

Clint thought as he sipped his coffee and shook his head.

"I'm not surprised. He wasn't much of anything but a troublemaker on the outskirts of Cochise County." As he spoke, Virgil picked up a spoon and stirred his coffee while staring down into it as though he could see the past reenacted in the dark liquid. "He tried robbing a few stagecoaches. Some say he even pulled a few jobs with Doc, but Wyatt would never believe a word of that."

"Sounds about right."

"Yeah, well it turns out Prouse is just the sort of asshole to lie about something like that to get a few more notches on his belt. He never actually got involved with our mess in Tombstone, but he did offer some outside assistance to the likes of Johnny Ringo and Ike Clanton. And that's just a fancy way of saying he hid them, fed them or worked as a spare gun hand when they needed it."

"I didn't know the Clantons had that many friends."

Virgil chuckled under his breath. "You'd be surprised. Some assholes still swear up and down that the Clantons and McLowerys were unarmed in that lot behind the OK Corral."

"So, since Wyatt was the only one to come out unscathed in that mess, I suppose he was the one who shot you, Morgan and Doc?"

"Told you they were assholes. Anyway, we had our fill of problems after that whole mess and they didn't stop after we got out of Tombstone. I took lead from a shotgun and Morgan . . ." As he said the name of his little brother, Virgil stared down at his coffee as if he was suddenly no longer sitting at that table.

Clint gave him a moment to deal with those ghosts, which was all Virgil needed. After clearing his throat and sipping his coffee, Virgil went on with an extra layer of steel beneath his voice.

"I've been moving right along with my life and making the best of what I've got. Wyatt's business interests rubbed off on me a bit, but I'll never be anything but a lawman when you come right down to it. I've tried talking sense into Wyatt till I'm blue in the face, but all that ever got me was a sore throat."

"Wyatt's been known to be a little stubborn," Clint said.

Virgil looked up at Clint as if he was about to laugh at that. Instead, he smirked and shook his head. "Wyatt's stubborn as a bull and when he's not tearing after the men that shot me and Morgan, he's trying to find out where those bastards are."

Narrowing his eyes a bit, Clint picked up on something in the older man's voice that didn't quite mesh with what he was saying. "So, you've just put it all behind you?" Clint asked. "What's done is done?"

Virgil didn't answer right away. He looked across at Clint with an equal amount of intensity. Grudgingly, he replied, "For the most part. I'm a lawman, Adams. I figure I'll cross paths with those bastards sooner or later, but that's not to say that I haven't done a bit of poking around."

"I see." Sensing that he was on the right track to uncovering more of the story surrounding his current situation, Clint asked, "How much poking around are we talking about?"

"Enough for me to find out that Xander Prouse was there the nights that me and Morgan were shot."

"Jesus."

Virgil nodded and kept his mouth shut as the server came back with Clint's breakfast. The woman hadn't been in Virgil's line of sight and she didn't walk with particularly heavy steps. She'd just been detected by the eyes that eventually grew in the backs of lawmen's heads.

She set down the plates she was carrying, asked if everyone was all right and then went about her business. The moment she was far enough away, Virgil started talking again.

"The men at the losing end of our dustup in Tombstone weren't content to scurry off with their tails tucked between their legs," Virgil said, referring to an already legendary gunfight as a mere dustup. "On the same note, they also didn't have as many people on their side any longer. They still had their supporters, but not half of them were so eager to take a stand against us and Holliday.

"When they decided to take cheap shots at me and Morgan, they needed to hire on some extra hands to do the job." When he sipped his coffee again, Virgil got a look on his face that would have been perfectly at home on the Reaper himself. "Lord knows those pricks were too yellow to come at an Earp without outnumbering him five to one."

From anyone else, that might have been considered nothing more than tough talk. From one of the Earp brothers, it was plain fact.

Glancing up as if he'd suddenly remembered Clint was sitting there, Virgil continued. "Xander Prouse was one of the first men the rest of those dogs went to so they could replenish their ranks. Since him and the assholes he works

with are still on the losing end of a fight they refuse to let
die, he's been taking it upon himself to take the fight to us.
Or, more specifically, to me."

"Why you in particular?" Clint asked.

"Because Morgan's dead and Wyatt's damn near impossi-
ble to find. Leastways, he is when he wants to be. He's got a
nose for sniffing out these dogs, and when he finds them,
they don't generally live to tell about it. And since I've gotten this," Virgil added while nodding down to his arm hanging in its sling, "those same dogs must see me as the easiest
target to pick off."

"That could be a painful mistake to make," Clint said.

"You're damn right it is. Prouse has been going around
and shooting up every business I've so much as lent money
to, leaving enough blood on the floor to paint a barn."

"Did Molly tell you about what she heard?" Clint asked.

"Yeah. She's a sweet little thing. I suppose she's the one
who heard about the asshole I got locked up in my jail right
now?"

Clint shrugged and got another forkful of breakfast down
before answering. "In a way. She said enough for me to figure out the men who shot up that store knew how close they
were to your jurisdiction."

"Close? Hell, they were *in* my jurisdiction."

"Either way, they knew all of that well enough. That
means they knew you'd come running once you heard about
what happened there. The only thing that made any sense
was that they made such a mess just to draw you out to that
trading post."

Virgil shook his head slowly. "That's a damn cold way to
operate."

"Maybe, but it's an efficient one. Sure got the job done."

Still shaking his head, Virgil chuckled slightly and said,
"Damn, Clint. It's a little scary how well you can think about
things as if you don't have a conscience."

"A necessary evil."

"Reminds me of Wyatt."

"I'll take that as a compliment. Anyway, if they wanted you to be at the trading post, that means they were either going to ambush you there or try to slip into Colton while you were gone."

"While the cat's away, huh?"

"Something like that," Clint replied. "Anyway, we made it without an ambush and that little girl heard them all ride away, so I thought I'd get back here as quick as I could."

"And you just happened to run into my new prisoner."

"That part was luck."

"Well," Virgil said as he lifted his coffee cup in a toast, "here's to that luck holding up a little while longer."

TWENTY

Lyssa had her hat pulled down low over her eyes and walked in a crouch so she could get a closer look at the ground. Even though she was already covered in dust and picking her way through a patch of bushes off to one side of a road, she had a smile on her face.

She was in her element and doing what she did best, without having to answer to anyone or worry about anybody looking over her shoulder.

Having ridden out of Colton at first light, she'd circled the town and found a small road leading in from the south. After picking up various traces that the road had been used fairly recently, she'd tied up her horse where it was out of sight and continued the rest of the way on foot.

The traces she'd found weren't much by most people's standards, but were just as good as paid advertisements to someone who knew what to look for. Since Lyssa Spencer had made her living as a tracker for several years, she most definitely knew what she was looking for.

Grinning victoriously, she reached out to push aside a few branches that appeared to have fallen along the side of the road. More likely, since there wasn't a tree to match those

branches within a few yards, someone had put those
branches there on purpose.

And if someone had put them there on purpose, that
meant they were trying to hide something.

And if they were trying to hide something, they weren't
exactly casual travelers.

While that simple line of reasoning flowed through her
head, Lyssa carefully moved aside the branches so she could
get a look at what was underneath. She hoped that, if she
was careful enough, she wouldn't disturb whatever it was the
others had been trying to hide.

"Ah," she whispered. "There you are."

Sure enough, there were several sets of tracks under the
branches. Since those tracks were set deep within the dirt,
that meant they must have been put there when the ground
was wet. She took a moment to think about when it had
rained last.

Although she couldn't think of a rain that had happened
within the last few weeks, the branches hadn't been broken
too long ago. After she'd gotten a good feel for which way
the tracks were headed, Lyssa placed the branches back in as
close to their original position as she could manage.

She was careful not to disturb those branches or any of
the bushes around them as she crept further down the trail
which forked off of the main road. Looking back toward the
road, she saw another good reason for those branches to be
there. To the casual eye, it seemed as though there was no
fork in the road at all. It was clever to try and hide the fork,
but they could have gone about the task in a much better
fashion.

Lyssa stayed low and kept moving in the direction of
those tracks. She didn't have to go for more than eighty yards
or so before she heard the crackle of a fire along with the
clang of metal against metal. After lowering herself onto her
belly and crawling forward a little ways more, she was able
to see the campfire as well as the men gathered around it.

The camp was set up against a boulder which was just tall

enough to act as cover so long as the men never stood up. By the way they were huddled over their tin plates and cups, it seemed as if they were more than accustomed to the inconvenience.

Lyssa counted three in all, but wasn't able to say if that was a final number. Hearing just enough over the crackle of the fire to tell that the men were whispering about something, she crawled forward a little ways more so she could try and pick up a word or two.

The camp was bristling with guns. There were rifles propped against the rocks, shotguns lying near the fire and pistols strapped around every man's waist. Although she'd seen the weapons, Lyssa didn't pay much attention to them after noting they were there. She patted the holster at her side to make certain her own gun was still in place and kept right on moving.

The closer she got without being noticed, the more confidence swelled up in her chest. A mischievous smile found its way to her face, as if she was creeping up on a group of boys who'd bullied her when she was a child.

That smile disappeared real quickly when one of the men snapped his eyes in her direction and plucked the gun from his holster.

"What was that?" the man hissed loud enough for even Lyssa to hear.

That was enough to put the rest of the men on their guard, and they immediately grabbed for the guns laying nearby.

Biting back the urge to swear under her breath, Lyssa began inching away from the camp and praying that she didn't make a noise loud enough to call down a storm of lead.

TWENTY-ONE

"So, what do you think of my friend Miss Spencer?"

Although that name sounded familiar, Clint wasn't able to place it right away when Virgil mentioned it. The two of them were walking along the boardwalk after a quick breakfast. Clint hooked his thumbs over his belt and pulled in a breath of fresh air to clear his thoughts. It only took a second or two, however, before the name struck the right chord in his brain.

"Oh, you mean Lyssa?" Clint asked.

"That's the one."

"She certainly knows what she's doing."

Virgil glanced over to Clint and stared at him just long enough for him to think the marshal knew about every meaning behind that phrase. Finally, Virgil nodded. "She's come in handy more than once. In fact, she's helped track down a couple other problems I've had since coming here and setting up shop."

"Did she help swing the vote to put that badge on your chest?"

"Not hardly, but she did help sniff out a few wanted men, which made me look pretty damn good. If she wasn't a

87

woman, I'd say she might have had a better shot at landing the job."

"Tracking them down is one thing," Clint pointed out. "Putting them away is another."

"Actually, I offered her a place with some more authority to it, but she refused. I think she didn't feel like putting up with all the sideways looks she'd get by doing the job better than plenty of men."

"Or she would just rather ride around in the open with nobody to answer to and no quotas to fill."

"I don't know about any quotas, but I do see your point. She is one of the more independent women I've met."

"And yet somehow you managed to get her to agree to work for a troublemaker like you."

Virgil smirked and straightened up as if he was proud to hold that title. "Troublemaking runs in the blood."

"That it does. And so does convincing otherwise sane people to follow you into battle."

While the posture remained the same, Virgil took on a bit more of a serious tone. "If I'd known of anyone else that would get the job done better, I would have asked them. But there's nobody better, Clint. This whole thing is coming to a boil and I'd prefer not to have another dustup like there was in Tombstone."

"It's gotten that bad?"

"It's about to. This Prouse fellow's got something to prove, and he doesn't mind spilling blood to prove it. You saw that much for yourself."

Clint thought back to the grisly scene at the trading post and nodded. Just remembering those bodies brought the stench of freshly spilled blood to his nose.

"I still don't know if he's trying to set things right in his own head or if he's trying to impress someone else," Virgil continued. "Maybe Wyatt was right and I should have been keeping up with this sort of thing the whole time. What it boils down to is that Prouse is a loose end that's set to do a lot more damage if it ain't tied up properly."

"There's plenty of loose ends from Tombstone," Clint said. "Believe me, whenever that many bad intentions are being tossed back and forth, there's going to be more loose ends than you could ever truly know." Stopping and facing Virgil directly, Clint patted the marshal on the shoulder and added, "Nobody could keep track of everything in a mess like that."

"I appreciate the thought, Clint, but it's my job to clean up as many of those messes as I can. Especially the ones that I had a hand in creating."

"Once again, spoken like a true lawman."

"Comes with the badge. While we're on the subject of badges, it might make things easier if you wore one for a stretch."

"You want to deputize me?"

"That way, I wouldn't have to take that pretty gun away from you or lock you up if you were forced into a rough situation."

"Oh yeah. Let's just hope that doesn't happen."

Even though he took the comments as lighthearted, Clint quickly saw that Virgil was as serious as the grave.

"It's been a while since I've worn a badge," Clint explained.

"It would only be temporary."

"But it's not really necessary."

"Actually," Virgil said, "it is. What's the matter, Clint? You have something against being a lawman for a little while?"

"Not at all. I just think I might be able to do more good if I'm independent. You know, so I'm not attached to you so directly."

Virgil chuckled and looked around as if he was including the entire world in what he said next. "By walking down the street and talking to me, you're going to be considered connected to me. That's how it's been since I've enforced the law, and it's even more so since everyone started picking sides in Tombstone."

"Fine. Deputize me. But what about Lyssa?"

"Same goes for her."

"You might want to reconsider that," Clint offered. "It may be too late for me in the eye of the public or anyone else who's watching, but she's kept more distance between herself and you. That is, as far as I know."

Virgil nodded. "I've used her for a few different jobs, but it's always been on a work-for-hire basis."

"Good. Keep her that way and she'll be able to make a move without everyone watching her and assuming she's moving on your behalf. It would sure make things easier if things do get rougher."

"If she wants to help out more than she's already done, then I'll take the same precautions with her," Virgil declared. "That includes deputizing her. That's how it's got to be if we're to keep on the right side of the law through this whole thing."

Clint winced slightly. "Actually, she does want to keep helping. What's more is that she's out there helping as we speak."

"Really? It's not anything dangerous, is it?"

TWENTY-TWO

Lyssa curled up in a ball, held her breath and kept praying for the man with the shotgun to walk by without noticing where she was.

She could hear the other men searching nearby.

In fact, a few of the others had already walked past her without looking down at the wrong moment to find her curled up and pressed against the base of a small tree. But the man that was close to her now was proving to be a real pain.

He wouldn't leave.

And he wouldn't stop staring at the ground and kicking at the bushes, as if he already knew where she was and had decided to play with her.

If he continued what he was doing for just another couple of seconds, he would undoubtedly spot her and kill her with one shot from the gun in his hands.

Well, if she was lucky, it might happen that quickly.

Before her imagination could run too far in the wrong direction, Lyssa heard those footsteps draw even closer to where she was hiding. She hadn't been in a whole lot of life-and-death situations, but she'd heard about how time seemed to slow down when one of them came.

This was one of those times.

She glanced around to try and catch sight of any of those others, and only spotted two more. Thankfully, they were far off and seemed to be headed away from her. That made her decision that much easier to make. When she saw that gunman moving toward her even quicker, Lyssa pulled in a breath and prepared herself to move.

Even though she was still wondering if she was doing the right thing, her body had already made the decision to spring. She pushed off on both legs and reached out with one hand. Lyssa didn't get a firm grip around the man's ankle, but she took him by such complete surprise that he wasn't able to get away from her before she could try again.

"What the hell?" he grunted as he stumbled back and looked down at the bushes he'd been about to pass.

Lyssa was a blur of motion as she finally managed to get a hold on the man's ankle and pull him forward while she continued to move ahead. Her other hand was wrapped around her pistol, which she used to smash into his shin.

Just as the man started to let out a pained grunt, he was being pulled off his balance and toppling toward the ground. By the time his back hit the dirt, it forced the air from his lungs, as well as the shout he'd been about to let fly.

Shocked that she'd brought the bigger man down, Lyssa wasted no time before crawling on top of him and dropping the butt of her pistol onto the man's chin.

She barely even realized what she was doing as she cracked him in the jaw. In fact, it seemed more like she was watching some crazy woman possessed by the devil beat the hell out of a man with her bare hands.

The pistol smashed into the man's face again and again until blood started to fly.

Still, the man squirmed and tried to shove her away, while bringing his own weapon around to get a shot at her. Even as his face became covered by a crimson mask, he still did his best to blink away the blood and point his gun at the wild thing that had attacked him.

A scream was at the back of Lyssa's throat as she antici-
pated the man's gun going off and killing her on the spot.
The more she hit him, the less it seemed to matter. On the
contrary, each blow she landed only stoked the angry fire in
the man's eyes.

She'd made a mistake.

That realization hit her like a cold slap in the face.

She'd made a fatal mistake and it was too late to do anything about it now.

Lyssa's next blow landed with a loud crunch.

This time, the butt of her gun seemed to have wedged
into the man's face. That was only because his face had
turned to one side and his nose caught on the edge of the pistol's grip. Once his face turned, he let out a breath and
stopped squirming.

For a moment, Lyssa wondered if she'd killed the man.
Then she heard him breathing and realized she'd somehow
managed to knock him out. Instead of celebrating her victory or even trying to figure out how she'd pulled it off, she
got to her feet and ran.

TWENTY-THREE

Clint had been around long enough to know that pacing a floor never made the clock tick any faster. Even so, after so much time had passed since he was supposed to meet up with Lyssa again, he couldn't help but pace to pass the time.

There were other things to do, but before he heard something from her, he knew he wouldn't be able to concentrate on much else. It was almost to the point where he was going to take Eclipse for a ride to try and find her himself when he saw a familiar face round the corner.

Clint was standing in front of the Prospector Hotel rather than inside of it, so he could spot Lyssa the moment she arrived for their meeting. When he actually saw her running down the street, he finally let out the breath he'd been holding.

Of course, the relief he felt didn't last long once he saw the almost frantic way in which she rushed down the street.

"What's the matter?" Clint asked once Lyssa was a bit closer. She didn't answer, and before he could ask again, he was being shoved toward the front door of the hotel.

Clint went along with her and stepped inside. She slammed the door and quickly went to one of the nearby windows so she could peek out while doing her best to stand away from the glass.

"Lyssa," Clint said sternly, "tell me what happened."

Her eyes darted in Clint's direction, but quickly went back to the street outside the window. "Has anything else happened since I left?"

"Like what?"

"I don't know. Shooting, shouting, a bunch of armed men coming through here like they were looking for someone?"

"What the hell have you been up to? I thought you were just going to scout the area outside of town."

"That's exactly what I did."

"So what's the problem?"

Lyssa let go of the curtain and flashed Clint a mischievous smile. "I found something."

"What did you find?"

"A camp. I think it belongs to those gunmen."

"Why do you think that? I'm sure there's plenty of camps around."

"This one was hidden and protected by enough guns to qualify it as a fort!"

Clint looked behind him and saw several people standing in the lobby, looking at him and Lyssa as if they were circus performers. Most of them were standing around the front desk, which was just far enough away for them to not have heard everything Lyssa said. Even so, the way she was talking was more than enough to draw some attention.

"Come on," Clint said as he took Lyssa's arm and pulled her away from the window.

As they walked past the desk, the clerk behind it held up a finger and said, "If you plan on using your room again, I'll have to insist that—"

"Don't worry about it," Clint said shortly and then steered Lyssa toward the small dining room that passed for a restaurant. Once he was inside, Clint went to a table in the corner and sat down so he could see the windows as well as the door leading back out to the lobby.

Reluctantly, Lyssa sat down as well.

"All right," Clint said. "Start at the beginning."

In an excited flurry of words, she told him about her scouting excursion, which led up to her discovery of the hidden fork in the road. When she started getting hung up on explaining the technical aspects of picking up and following the trail, Clint had to put her back on the more important subject.

"You said there was a camp?" he asked.

"Yes, I was just getting to that. It was set up in a perfect spot, but I'm sure I could find it again."

"How many men were there?"

"I'm not sure."

"What do you mean you're not sure?"

She blinked a few times and said, "Like I told you. I'm not sure. I know I saw at least three or four of them, but that was before they started chasing me."

"You mean they spotted you?"

"No! Well . . . I don't think they did."

Clint had to laugh and shake his head at what he was hearing. "I thought you were the expert tracker here."

"I am! I didn't have any trouble tracking them from town back to their camp. The trouble started after I tried to get in closer. Usually I'm not the one doing all the fighting."

Taking a look at her, Clint said, "At least you don't look hurt."

"I'm not," Lyssa replied with a wide grin. "But I sure came awfully close."

"Let's hear it."

From there, she went on to tell him all about nearly being captured by the gunmen as she hid in the bushes. Her words came out of her in a constant flow and didn't stop until she was finished telling him how she managed to get away from the one man who'd gotten close to discovering her.

"Sounds to me like you got awfully lucky," Clint said once she finally stopped to catch her breath.

"Lucky? Is that what you call it when you manage to get away from a situation like that?"

"I don't get into situations like that," he lied. "In fact, I don't think I like where this whole thing is headed."

"Why not? You wanted me to find out where they went after leaving town and I did. The rest was a bit unexpected, but I got away all right and I know I wasn't followed."

"I'm talking about more than just today," Clint explained. "I mean this whole thing. Virgil filled me in on some of what is behind all of this and something still doesn't set right."

"Like what?"

"I don't know yet."

"Is there anything I can do?" When she asked that question, Lyssa saw something in Clint's eyes that made her lean forward expectantly. "Come on. There's something else I can do. I can tell."

"I'm not sure if it'll go over too well or not."

The excited flare in her eyes had returned, and Lyssa was practically perched upon the edge of her seat in anticipation of what Clint was going to say. "I may not have been there to see those bodies at that trading post, but I heard all about it. If there's anything I can do to bring in the animals that were behind that carnage, I want to do it."

"I know, but . . ."

"Clint," she interrupted with a gentle tone in her voice while reaching out to put her hand on his arm. "Anything."

Placing his own hand on top of hers, Clint thought it over for another few seconds before giving her a few soft pats. He then leaned forward and whispered into her ear.

He only whispered to her for a few seconds before leaning back again so he could look her in the eyes and await her response.

Lyssa leaned back a bit with subtle surprise written on her face. Once she'd allowed Clint's words to sink in, she pulled her hand out from under Clint's and used it to smack him across the face. She didn't say another word as she shot up from her chair and stormed out of the hotel.

TWENTY-FOUR

Jeff Conway sat in the opposite corner from where Clint and Lyssa were located in the restaurant inside the Prospector Hotel. Even though he'd been ordered not to wear all the guns that were as much a part of him as his own limbs, he'd considered wearing them anyway. Without the weight of all that iron hanging on him, he felt more vulnerable than if he was naked.

But now he saw the sense in that order Prouse had given.

Not only was he able to move around without attracting so much attention, but he could blend in a whole lot better than when he was armed for war.

The starched shirt he'd bought just for this occasion didn't itch so much now that he'd finally seen something to make all the waiting and sneaking around worthwhile.

At first, he'd thought it was enough to catch a glimpse of Clint and Lyssa inside the hotel. Just knowing where they were staying could be an advantage if things got pushed far enough. But when he saw that woman slap Clint across the face and leave, Jeff had to fight from laughing out loud.

He was downright proud of himself that he not only kept quiet, but managed to look as though he was still more interested in picking at the stack of pancakes that had been sitting in front of him long enough to get colder and less appetizing than a pile of oven mitts.

From the corner of his eye, Jeff watched as Clint sat at his table for a few more moments, until the other folks stopped glancing over at him. By then, those folks were distracted by the slam of the hotel's front door as Lyssa completed her exit.

Clint still sat there like a dejected puppy and offhandedly waved away the server who came over to ask what he wanted to eat.

Jeff kept his head down as he got up and paid his bill. From there, he walked calmly outside to try and see if he could make out where Lyssa had gone.

There was no trace of her.

By then, there was more than enough commotion on the streets of Colton to swallow up one angry woman. Jeff looked around for a little while, but quickly realized that she could have gone any number of directions and it was useless to try and guess which one. Despite that, he still had one hell of a grin on his face as he made his way back to the Rusty Nail Saloon.

The saloon was less than half-full and most of the traffic was centered around the card games being played throughout the place. Jeff skirted those tables and headed for a narrow staircase that led up to the rooms that were mostly occupied by the working girls there.

Having lingered for a moment or two to listen to one of the louder girls at work in the neighboring room, Jeff finally knocked upon the door at the end of the hall. It came open just enough to show one eye as well as one gun barrel. Jeff looked into the eye impatiently before the door came open the rest of the way.

"I thought you weren't to come back until later," Prouse said as he holstered his gun and stepped aside so Jeff could enter.

"Yeah, yeah. I thought you'd want to hear this."

"Hear what?"

Jeff walked over to the bed, reached under it and fished out one of several gunbelts stashed under there. After buckling his guns around his waist, he sat on the edge of the bed and faced a very anxious Prouse.

"Hear what?" Prouse snarled. "You won't like what happens if I have to ask again."

Even that threat couldn't put a dent in the already crooked smile on Jeff's face. "I saw Adams and the bitch."

"You did? Where?"

"At the same hotel that deputy recommended to Hobbes."

"I knew it! That cocksucker Earp just can't abide missing one opportunity to put another few cents into his pocket. So he's staying there?"

"I guess so. What's even better is that Adams was talking to Marshal Earp earlier today, and it looked like he was telling that bitch all about it. Now we know where to find both of them, and we only need one to talk for us to know just what Earp's doing about them messages we've been sending."

Prouse nodded to himself. "This is turning out even better than I'd hoped."

TWENTY-FIVE

A few minutes later, the room was stuffed full of armed men.

Actually, besides Prouse and Jeff, there were only three others in there. Being a room normally used for less than an hour at a time, it wasn't much bigger than a large dressing room. The men gathered in there as a fresh customer knocked against the wall next door and the unenthusiastic cries of a working girl started to drift through the air.

"Looks like we were right about that hotel, Hobbes," Prouse said.

The big man nodded from where he was leaning against the wall. "All them Earps are pimps. They hustle just like any other pimp and that includes steering folks so they can spend their money in the right places."

"Well, Adams isn't the only one there. That tracker working for Earp was there too. After we lost track of that bitch, I thought she'd slipped us for good."

"Not hardly," Jeff said. "And it gets better."

"Since we're all here, explain it to us."

Jeff nodded and rubbed his hands together as if he'd finally been given permission to take a slice of the pie he'd been eyeing. "Them two were in the hotel getting something to eat. She was excited about something or other."

"What was she excited about?" Hobbes asked.

"I couldn't hear," Jeff said dismissively. "But I sure as hell heard when she slapped him across the face and walked off on him."

The expression on Prouse's face shifted from anxious to confused. "Why would she do that?"

"Whatever it was, it pissed her off something terrible. Pissed her off so bad that she up and left. Everyone in that place was watching. It was a hell of a scene."

Prouse scratched his chin and paced to the other side of the room. "I know that Earp is old-fashioned about working with women. I've even heard that he doesn't get along too well with them in the professional sense."

"Hell yes," Hobbes grunted. "Some of the whores in Tombstone said he was a real bastard to work with."

"That could have come from any number of things. That's not what I'm talking about. She was working with Marshal Earp before Adams came along, so she's probably upset about the new arrangement. It's just Earp's style to let Adams deliver the bad news so he didn't look bad himself."

"It'd be tough to look any worse than Adams did in that dining room today," Jeff said.

After thinking about it a few seconds longer, Prouse grumbled and turned back around so he was facing the others. "It's a waste of time to try and figure all of this out right now. The important thing is that she's pissed at him, which probably means she's pissed at them both. What we need to do next is make certain of that for ourselves."

"I lost sight of her after she stormed out of there."

"Then you'll just have to find her," Prouse declared.

"Me? Why me? I was gonna say one of these others should do it. I've had my fill of sneaking around." When he didn't see any accommodating faces around him, Jeff added, "What about one of the men camping outside of town? They ain't even been seen around here yet."

"And that's how it's going to stay. Those men are staying

outside of town until they're needed and they won't come in a moment before. You're the one that's going."

Jeff rolled his eyes and clenched his jaw, knowing all too well how useless it was to argue after an order had been handed down.

"While I'm sure you did your best to keep your head down in that restaurant," Prouse explained, "you still might have been spotted. It just makes sense for you to approach her, since you won't have to lie about overhearing her little scuffle with Adams."

"I guess that makes sense," Jeff sighed.

"Besides," Hobbes grunted, "you're the one that let her get out of your sight, so you're the one that should find her again."

"What do I do once I found her?"

"She's been working with Earp, so she must know something about what he intends to do now that Adams is here."

Hobbes had yet to move from the spot he'd taken at the beginning of the meeting, but he still seemed to fill more than half the room. "Find out what happened to Bill," he said. "Nobody else has heard or seen anything of him since we sent him here. Since that bitch is so close to Adams and Earp, she's got to know something."

"Bill's in jail," one of the other men said.

When they heard that, everyone else in the room turned to stare at the man as if they hadn't even realized he was there at all. In response, the man simply shrugged.

"What?" the man asked, since he was already used to being ignored. "I thought we all knew that. All anyone had to do was read a newspaper."

Jeff grinned in a way that made it appear the scar running across his chin was grinning as well. "There now," he said. "That's why we have someone else besides Hobbes at these goddamn powwows."

"What else did the newspaper say?" Hobbes asked.

"Just that he was in jail for fighting."

"When's the trial?"

The man shrugged. "Didn't say."

"She'll know," Prouse said. "And since there's nothing more constant in this world than an angry woman, I know she'll be willing to talk to anyone that'll listen. While you're talking to her, Jeff, see what it was that got her so riled up."

Jeff let out a snorting chuckle. "That should be easy."

"I still don't see the use in all this pussyfooting around," Hobbes snarled. "We're here, so why don't we just walk up and blow that goddamn Earp to hell?"

Prouse wheeled around to stare the bigger man directly in the eyes. "Because I saw what happened to the last bunch of men who tried to have a straight-up fight with the Earps. Now that this one's aligned himself with Clint Adams, he's got an even bigger ace in the hole than they had with Doc Holliday."

Looking around at the men gathered in that room, Prouse said, "This cocksucker's gonna get what's coming to him, but we need to tie up all these loose ends in one shot because we won't get another."

"Don't forget," Hobbes growled. "Adams is mine."

Prouse nodded. "We do this right, and it'll be like taking candy from a baby."

TWENTY-SIX

Clint stormed into Virgil's office and slammed the door behind him. The men inside the office had such frayed nerves already that most of them reflexively grabbed for their guns when they heard the sudden sound. The only one who didn't try to draw was Virgil himself.

In fact, he looked like the most collected of all of them, including Clint. "What's all the fuss about?" Virgil asked.

"Lyssa's gone," Clint replied.

Rising to his feet, Virgil had a look on his face that could have sent someone directly to their grave. "What happened to her?"

"Nothing like that. She just left. She doesn't want any part of working with us. Well," Clint added, "she doesn't want to work with me anymore."

Virgil let out the breath he'd been holding and lowered himself back into his chair. He winced and shifted in his seat so most of the weight was being supported by his right side rather than his left. "Are you talking about that quarrel you had at the Prospector?"

"You heard about that?" Clint asked, genuinely surprised.

Virgil nodded. "It is my place, Clint. Besides, I hear she

smacked you so hard that it could have been heard outside. What the hell did you say to her, anyhow?"

Clint rolled his eyes and shook his head. "Never mind about that. What's important for you to know is that she's out."

"If that's the way it's got to be. Besides," he added with a wink, "I'm sure I'll hear all about it before too long."

Clint didn't have any doubt about that. In fact, he wouldn't be surprised if Virgil knew even more before the day was out. But there were still too many things to do before he worried about that. "She did give me a report before she stormed off, however."

"A report?" Virgil asked. "From what?"

"From the scouting run I sent her on this morning." When he saw the hackles raise on the back of the marshal's neck, Clint quickly acted to douse the flames. "This was before our conversation this morning, Virgil. Back when I thought I could help out a friend without needing to be sworn in."

"It's the way the law works, Clint. It's not just something I came up with."

"Do you want to hear about what she found, or do I need to be wearing a badge to continue with this conversation?"

Even though Clint had been partly kidding about that, Virgil responded by snapping his fingers and pointing to him. Almost instantly, one of the deputies stepped forward with one hand extended. Sure enough, when Clint looked down at that hand, he saw a dented badge in it.

"Don't look so surprised, Clint," Virgil said. "I aim to keep this legal and this is the best way."

Clint took the badge and pinned it to his shirt. "Any more formalities?"

"Yes, but we can skip 'em. Consider yourself sworn in. Now, what did Lyssa find while she was out and about?"

Clint sat down at one of the desks, as if he was claiming it for his own. "She found a camp outside of town. She said it was hidden away pretty well and the men camping there were armed to the teeth."

"Do we know for certain these are the same fellows we're after?"

"It's a pretty safe bet, unless you know about some other gangs that are planning to raid Colton. As far as I know, there's no other reason for men like that to be hiding out and waiting for something."

"That's true," Virgil admitted, "but I'd like to know for sure. Did she tell you where to find the camp?"

Clint nodded. "I could probably get there on my own."

"That's good, but you won't be on your own. Take a few men with you to watch your back."

"Actually, I should be fine going it alone."

Virgil shook his head. "I know you can handle yourself, Clint, but I've seen what can happen if someone gets in a lucky shot." As he said that, Virgil squirmed and shifted the arm in his sling. "I appreciate all you're doing here, but I'm not going to take unnecessary risks."

Clint looked around at the deputies. For the most part, they all seemed levelheaded and strong. They were also quite eager at the prospect of being chosen to go with him to this camp. Getting up from his chair, Clint walked over to Virgil's desk and spoke in a lower voice.

"I know you've only picked good men to work with you," Clint said. "This isn't against them, but I still think I'd be better off on my own."

Virgil met Clint's gaze and didn't even flinch at his concerns. "Then at least take one with you. This kid's got a nose like a bloodhound and he ain't trigger happy. Reminds me a bit of you, except for the part about not being trigger happy."

Lately, Virgil's attempts at humor were so far apart that they always took Clint by surprise. Even so, the sly grin was a welcome addition to the older man's weathered face.

"Where is he?" Clint asked.

"Right behind you," Virgil replied while shifting around to nod to one of the other men in the room.

Clint turned to get a look at who was going to be his partner and saw a short man in his late twenties step forward.

The man had tussled blond hair and a pockmarked face. He extended his hand and gave Clint a slow nod.

The part that Clint found odd was that he didn't recall the shorter man even being in that room until Virgil had pointed him out. For that reason alone, Clint figured he wasn't such a bad choice for a partner after all.

"This is Michael," Virgil said.

Michael shook Clint's hand with a confident grip and only mumbled one word by way of a hello.

"Good to meet you, Michael," Clint said. "I assume you know me already?"

"Sure do."

"Good. I hope you're ready for a ride."

Michael smirked and nodded with a bit more enthusiasm. "Sure am."

TWENTY-SEVEN

Jeff tugged at the collar of his starched shirt and cursed under his breath. By having the damned thing buttoned so close to his neck, he got a real good idea of what it must have felt like to be strung up by a lynch mob. When he saw someone looking in his direction, he did his best to force a smile onto his face and act civil.

Judging by the uncomfortable nods he got in return, Jeff wasn't doing too good a job at putting folks at ease.

"Eh, to hell with 'em," he muttered while popping open the button at his collar and nearly ripping the shirt in the process. Although he looked something less than civil, he was able to breathe again.

As soon as he was able to take a breath without wheezing, Jeff saw the very person he'd been waiting for.

Lyssa walked past the front door of the Prospector and stopped as if she was thinking about going inside. She paused, turned her back on the place and then kept walking. Jeff took off after her. He was almost running at first, but then slowed up a bit so he didn't overtake her quite so suddenly.

"'Scuse me, ma'am," Jeff said once he caught up to her.

Lyssa didn't respond until Jeff raised his voice and repeated himself. Even then, she barely seemed to hear him at all. When she got a look at him coming up behind her, she took a quick step in the opposite direction.

"Sorry. I didn't mean to startle you."

"What do you want?" she asked.

"I . . . uh . . . just wanted to make sure you were all right."

She furrowed her brow a bit and took another step away from him. "Yes. I'm fine. Thanks for asking." With that, she turned and continued walking down the street.

It was a busy time of day, when folks were moving about in Colton at a brisk pace. The streets were narrow, which made them seem even more crowded since they were that much easier to fill. Horses and wagons rumbled along at a snail's pace as people moved on either side of, and sometimes between, them.

This time, Jeff wasn't so worried about appearances as he bolted after Lyssa and took hold of her arm. When she turned around again, she tore her arm free and fixed a fiery stare upon him.

"I don't know who you are," she snarled, "but I'd suggest you leave me alone if you want to stay healthy."

Jeff held up his hands and gave her some room. Unlike the last few minutes, he didn't have to try to put a grin on his face. Seeing the way Lyssa handled herself and glared at him was more than enough to make him smile.

"Like I said, I just wanted to be sure you were doing all right," he assured her.

"Just who the hell are you?" Lyssa asked.

"My name's Jeff. I was eating at the Prospector earlier today when you had your little . . . uh . . . disagreement."

Some of the anger faded from her eyes as she slowly started to nod. "You heard that, huh?"

"Heard and saw it. I was sitting at my table when you hauled off and nearly knocked that poor soul out of his chair."

Lyssa laughed and stepped aside as a line of people tried to get past her so they could get to a nearby row of shops.

"That might be a small exaggeration, but I see your point. Actually, I'm doing just fine."

"Well, a gentleman can never be too certain. That fellow looked awfully mad when he watched you leave."

"Did he, now?"

"Oh yes. That's why I thought to myself that I wished I would have gone after you to make sure he didn't try anything."

"Try anything?" Lyssa asked. "Like what?"

"You never know, ma'am. I do know he was wearing a gun and looked more than riled up enough to use it."

Lyssa looked stunned as she thought that over. So stunned, in fact, that the next couple that tried to walk past her almost knocked her off the boardwalk. When she shook herself back into the present, Lyssa sputtered and tried to find the words to express what she was thinking.

"I . . . didn't know he was that angry," was the best she could come up with under the circumstances.

"Well, believe it. Actually, since I stayed behind, I could hear him saying something to the effect of wishing he could get his hands on you for slapping him the way you did."

Lyssa's frown grew even more. "That's terrible."

"Especially since he must have said something awful to get you to do that in the first place."

That was more than enough to snap her back into focus. In fact, she seemed to flare up a little more than when she'd been grabbed by Jeff a minute ago.

"If you don't mind me asking," Jeff said sheepishly, "what did he say to you back there?"

"Something that earned him the slap that I gave him."

"Would it have anything to do with Marshal Earp, by any chance?"

"What do you know about that?" she asked.

"To be honest, I represent some gentlemen who were hired by the marshal's family to look after him."

"I've worked with Marshal Earp and he never mentioned anything like this."

"Of course. That's because he doesn't know about it. Just like he doesn't know about the men trying to do him harm."

"What men?"

"Have you heard about that terrible business at the trading post?"

"You mean the shootings?"

"It was more like a slaughter," Jeff said. "The devils behind that are making their way into Colton. They're the cowardly sort who have sent scouts ahead to get close to the marshal so they can finish the job they started years ago. They've hired someone to spy on Marshal Earp, and I fear he might have fooled you as well."

"This is a lot to take in."

"I know, but you might be more help to us than you realize." Leaning in so he could whisper to her, Jeff added, "Clint Adams is the spy we're after."

TWENTY-EIGHT

Fortunately for both Lyssa and Jeff, the Rusty Nail wasn't far from where they'd had their initial conversation. Jeff did his best to fill the walk with small talk, but wound up struggling so much that he was quickly reduced to a grumbling string of chatter.

Unfortunately for Lyssa, she was forced to listen to him every step of the way.

They stepped into the saloon as more patrons were starting to trickle in. It was bound to get much more crowded in a matter of hours, but just then they had no trouble at all spotting Prouse at his table in the back.

Dressed in a sharp suit and freshly shaved, Prouse stood up the moment he saw Lyssa approach. He extended his hand to her and introduced himself in a smooth voice. "I'm Allan Woodward," he told her.

"Lyssa Spencer."

"Pleased to meet you. Take a seat."

Lyssa sat down and was sure to keep the two men in her sight. "I don't really know why I'm here," she said.

"You happen to be fortunate enough to have my associate staying in your hotel," Prouse said. "Actually, that's not a mistake. You see, we've been following Mr. Adams for some time."

"I was told that he's supposed to be a spy or something?"

"In a manner of speaking. Actually, he's more of an assassin. I know that sounds rather dramatic, but he is a killer. In fact, he's a killer who's fairly well known. He's also known as The Gunsmith."

Lyssa nodded while still shifting her eyes between the two men in front of her. "I've heard him called that."

"Then you must also know he didn't get that name for being a craftsman."

"Well, actually—"

"He's a killer, ma'am," Prouse interrupted. "Plain and simple."

"So what does this have to do with me?"

"Well, it seems that he's shown his true colors and you rightfully put him in his place. Would you mind letting me know what started that fight?"

Letting out a heavy sigh, Lyssa said, "That's between me and him."

"Of course it is." Prouse leaned forward and lowered his voice a bit. "He probably asked you to do something inappropriate, didn't he?"

"Yes, but that's not too hard to figure out."

Prouse nodded. "Adams has used plenty of women the same way. He gets close to them, sometimes even takes them to his bed, and then works his way in even closer." As he spoke, Prouse watched Lyssa's face carefully. He could see a subtle twitch at the corner of her eye, which told him he was on the right track.

"That's how he operates," Prouse continued. "He's asked women to do plenty of things for him, but it's all so he can get closer to his target."

"Clint's already close to Marshal Earp. So am I."

"The most dangerous kinds of snakes are the ones right under your feet."

"I still think you're wrong about Clint."

"Why's that?"

"Because he didn't ask me to do anything that would put Marshal Earp in danger. He's trying to help him."

"What did he say, then?"

"He said he didn't want me to ride alongside of him or anyone else helping the marshal, but that I could stick around and keep him company at night."

"That's terrible," Prouse said. "But did he mention exactly when he wanted you to keep him company?"

"What does that matter?"

"Because I think he's setting you up to take a fall for him, ma'am. A very big fall. Making certain you're in the right spot at the right time will make it much easier for him to do his own dirty business and then point the finger at you."

"That's ridiculous!" Lyssa said as she pushed away from the table and got to her feet. "Why the hell would Clint want to set me up?"

"Someone could be blamed for breaking a man out of jail this very evening," Prouse quickly said.

Those words stopped Lyssa in her tracks and put a shocked look on her face. Although she tried to talk, no sounds came out of her mouth. When she felt Jeff's hand on her arm, she allowed herself to be lowered back into her chair.

"You mean that man who was caught running out of this saloon?" she asked.

"That's the one. We know for a fact that Adams wants to get that man out of jail and that he was arranging to have someone waiting to be caught and killed so none of the blame would come around to him."

"That's terrible."

"It sure is, but it doesn't have to happen like that if you help me and my men stop him."

"What do you want from me?"

"Since Adams is working with Marshal Earp, he'll know about all the men working as deputies, the marshal's personal habits, where he keeps his records, that sort of thing.

Those are the spots where he'll want to hit Marshal Earp. Since I gather you're close to the marshal already, you could fill me in on these things so we can stay one step ahead of this heartless assassin who's already signed your death warrant."

Lyssa stared straight ahead as the color drained from her face

"You look like you need a drink," Prouse said.

"Yes," she replied. "That would be nice."

Prouse snapped his fingers and shooed Jeff away to fetch the drink. Since the job required going to the bar, Jeff was more than happy to oblige. He walked to the far end of the bar, where Hobbes just happened to be standing.

TWENTY-NINE

"You really think she's buying any of this?" Jeff asked.

Hobbes chuckled and shook his head. "Hell if I know, but watching this is the most fun I've had in a hell of a long time. What's he trying to do, again?"

"He still wants to see about getting some information out of her."

"What the hell could she know that we need so badly, anyway? I still say the only thing that needs to be done is walk into that marshal's office and fill it full of lead."

"Something about getting more bees with honey," Jeff grumbled. Looking over his shoulder, he saw Prouse leaning forward to pat Lyssa on the shoulder while whispering in her ear. He turned back to Hobbes and said, "I actually think he's getting somewhere with her. Maybe he was right and Adams really did piss her off."

"That don't make this a brilliant plan." Hobbes slapped the top of the bar and pointed to his glass.

The barkeep filled the glass with whiskey and was about to leave when he was collared by Jeff. He got the other two drinks as quickly as he could so he could find somewhere else to be.

Hobbes downed his whiskey while staring disgustedly at

119

Prouse. "I can't believe Johnny Ringo ever had anything to do with that fucking idiot."

"Ringo needed a place to hole up as well as some reinforcements from time to time. Prouse got in over his head and wound up setting his friends up for a fall. I guess I can see why he wants the Earps dead."

"He got a few dollars thrown his way when he let one of those cowboys hide out at his place when the Earps made things too hot for them in town," Hobbes said. "Sure, some of Prouse's partners got killed along the line, but that's only because they were dumber than he was."

Shaking his head at the charade going on over at the table where Lyssa was sitting, Jeff muttered, "Hard to imagine anyone much dumber than this."

Hobbes leaned against the bar and watched the rest of the world go by like it was a show. "You know what a figure-head is?"

Jeff turned to look at Hobbes as if the other man had sprouted horns. "Huh? You mean those wooden statues at the front of a boat?"

"That's them."

"What's that got to do with anything?"

"Those statues are at the front so they can take all the damage while the rest of the boat sails on." Hobbes rubbed his finger along the inside of the empty whiskey glass and lifted it to his nose. "I should say, while the more important part of the boat sails on."

Glancing back at Prouse, who sat at his table wearing his new suit the way a bad actor wore an ill-fitting costume, Jeff saw plenty of sense in those words. "He's been doing a hell of a job so far. I mean, the raids have been moving like clockwork."

"Because they weren't his idea," Hobbes said.

"Whose were they? Yours?"

Rather than answer that question directly, Hobbes kept his eyes steady and let a fraction of a smirk crawl onto his face. "You know my history just like you know his. Who do you think could get a raid to go off that smoothly?"

Before Jeff could answer, Hobbes asked, "Remember how squeamish he was at the beginning when we had to kill that saloon owner's family as well as the owner himself?"

Even though it had been a while since that instance, the mere mention of it brought an immediate reaction to Jeff's face. "Yeah."

"Did you notice how I've had to step up and take the lead when all the real killing's been done? I mean, Prouse has spilled his share of blood, but he just don't have what it takes to kill an Earp. Not even a crippled one."

"Goddamn," Jeff breathed. "Am I glad to hear that. I was starting to think I was taking orders from a crazy man."

"He's not crazy," Hobbes said. "Just stupid. I needed him because there's no way I'd get this close to Earp if he knew I was coming. I couldn't set him up just right without doing everything we've done."

"But what about all of this?" Jeff asked while waving to the table at the other end of the room.

"This is what happens when you let the figurehead steer the ship for a few hours."

"Should I put a stop to it?" Jeff asked hopefully.

"Nah. If he can get her to talk voluntarily, that's fine. If not, I'll take a run at her myself. Either way, it doesn't really matter. That little lady won't be alive to see the outside of this saloon again. I don't even want to worry about that until I get back from the jailhouse. After that, I doubt anyone will miss one pretty little scout."

THIRTY

Clint and Michael rode out like a fire had been set behind them. Although the horse Michael rode wasn't quite fast enough to keep up with Eclipse, it was close enough to cover plenty of ground in a real short amount of time. Without one word passing between them, they bolted out of town and headed straight for the spot that Lyssa had described earlier.

The only reason Clint spotted the fork in the road was that Lyssa had described it so well to him before. Even then, when he signaled for them to come to a stop, Clint wondered if he'd even picked the right spot.

The bushes looked as though they hadn't been disturbed, and the ruts in the road weren't even broken. Clint took Lyssa at her word and got down to get a closer look at the spot for himself. Sure enough, after a bit of poking around, he saw the branches that had been laid out to cover the very marks Lyssa had described.

Looking up at the younger deputy, Clint asked, "Did you know about this trail?"

"Nope."

"Stay here." With that, Clint moved past the bushes and over to the top of a hill which dropped down to a rock formation that also fit within Lyssa's description.

Clint kept himself low and moved as fast as he could while also keeping as quiet as possible. In a matter of seconds, he disappeared from Michael's view.

Just as the deputy was about to go after Clint anyway, he saw something moving toward the bushes. A few seconds later, Clint rushed over to Eclipse and reached for the rifle strapped to the Darley Arabian's saddle.

"There's a camp all right," Clint said as he took hold of the rifle and checked it over.

"How many?" Michael asked.

"I counted three, but there's probably more. I didn't stay long enough to get a very good look."

"Why not?"

"Because we're heading right back over there," Clint replied with a grin.

Two men sat by the sputtering campfire while another searched through a bag of supplies. Even though their eyes were open, they looked more like they were asleep. All of them had long faces and bags under their eyes. The expressions they wore were almost comical masks of boredom.

"How much longer do we gotta stay out here?" one of the men asked.

The one foraging through the supplies answered, "Until we get the call to come into town." Suddenly, his eyes lit up as he pulled a small bag of coffee from the sack. "Looks like there's more in here after all."

"We've been out here for too long."

"We knew it was coming. We drew the short straws, so . . ."

The man trailed off as he heard something that made his ears prick up like a dog's. All of the others must have heard it as well, since they immediately grabbed for their guns and jumped to their feet.

Just then, the sound of a running horse drifted through the air, causing all the men to turn in that direction. That way, Clint was able to walk right up to the camp without being spotted.

"Hello there," Clint said in a friendly voice.

"Who the hell are you?" one of the men asked.

"I'm just passing through. I thought I could borrow some coffee."

For a moment, none of the men knew what to think. Then, one of them squinted as his eyes found the badge pinned to Clint's chest. "You a lawman?"

"For the time being. Is that a problem?"

After passing a few quick glances back and forth between one another, the men brought their guns to bear upon Clint and tightened their fingers on their triggers.

The moment he saw that movement, Clint dropped to one knee and drew the Colt from its holster. He fired his first shot at the man closest to him, who was wielding a shotgun. The shotgun roared, but only after the man holding it had caught some lead himself and was toppling over backward.

Buckshot flew over Clint's head, but even that wasn't enough to distract him as he picked his next target and fired. This shot creased the elbow of one of the men carrying a rifle, causing him to drop his weapon as his entire arm went numb.

Before the third man at the campfire could get a shot off, the horse they'd heard a few moments ago charged toward him and Michael fired a shot from his saddle. The round caught the man in the chest just as he was about to blast the deputy's horse. He hit the ground and squirmed, but soon stopped moving altogether.

Before Clint could move from his spot, he heard a voice coming from the rocks at the opposite side of the camp.

"Toss that gun! Right now!"

Clint looked over to see another dirty face staring back at him over the barrel of a Winchester rifle. Since he was already in the other man's sights, he opened his fingers and let the Colt fall to the ground.

"I've got him covered," the deputy said.

"Take yer shot, lawman," the gunman with Clint in his sights replied. "Because if you even think about pulling that trigger, I'll send your friend here to hell."

Before either of the two men could continue their threats, Clint said, "He's right, Michael. Lower the gun."

Reluctantly, the deputy complied.

"See?" Clint said. "We can be reasonable. Now how about you tell me what your men are doing out here and why you opened fire on us like that."

"To hell with you!"

"Would it make a difference if I told you Xander Prouse was already in Marshal Earp's custody?"

"You're lying."

"How do you think we found this camp?"

The gunman looked as if he'd been kicked in the gut. He began shifting on his feet while his breaths came in short gulps. "He wouldn't do that."

To Clint, the gunman sounded like a bad card player trying to pass off a pair of threes as a full house. "Earp's got him in custody and he handed you over as part of a deal. He told us we should come in blasting and not listen to a word you said about it."

"That's bullshit! All we were doing out here was waiting!"

"Waiting for what?" Clint asked.

Before the man could answer, another figure approached the camp and caught Michael's eye.

"Look out!" the deputy shouted as he lifted his gun and took aim at the new arrival.

The man was obviously another one of the campers, and he wasted no time before taking a shot at Michael. The deputy responded by pulling his trigger, but he missed his target.

Clint waited for the man aiming at him to look away, giving him enough time to snap his foot straight up and pop his rifle into the air. The gun had been laying across his boot the entire time, waiting for such a moment. Clint grabbed it out of the air and sent a single round through the other man's skull.

Since the new arrival was still standing, Clint shifted his aim in that direction. From the corner of his eye, he could see Michael crumple over and onto the back of his horse's neck.

The moment he saw a gun being aimed at him, Clint shifted and fired using nothing but reflex and instinct. His shot snapped the gunman's head back to fill the air behind him with a spray of dark red pulp. The gunman dropped like a sack of flour and didn't move again.

Walking over to the man he'd wounded, Clint shouted, "You still with me, Michael?"

For a sickening moment, there was nothing but silence.

Then, Michael slowly tried to straighten up. He was holding his side when he said, "I'll be all right."

Clint stared along the top of his rifle, which was pointed directly at the gunman with the wounded elbow. There was a fire in Clint's eyes that had been ignited by the thought of Michael being killed.

"This is your lucky day, asshole," Clint said. "If my partner there was dead, you'd be looking the devil in the eye right about now. If you tell me everything you know about what Prouse has got planned, I might just settle for hauling you in alive."

The gunman looked around warily. When he saw nobody coming to his aid, he groaned, "All right, all right. I'll talk. Just get me out of here."

"Talk first," Clint snarled. "Then we'll see if you get to leave this spot."

THIRTY-ONE

Lyssa knew she was in trouble.

She knew that much the moment she saw Xander Prouse sit in front of her while trying to pass himself off as someone else. Although she didn't know why he was going through the act at first, it soon became clear what he was trying to get out of her. It was also clear that he didn't realize she'd followed him from his secret camp outside of town a few hours before dawn.

While trying to maintain the appearance of being upset and close to tears, Lyssa looked around the saloon for any more signs of trouble. It didn't take long before she spotted a few more rough-looking men watching her from various spots throughout the room.

She was most definitely in trouble.

"I need to get up for a moment," she said.

Prouse was still sitting in front of her, thinking he was tricking her into giving information when she'd actually been feeding him tidbits that didn't mean much of anything.

"Anything you want, I can get for you," Prouse said with a fair attempt at a cordial smile.

"I could use some water, but I'll get it myself. I really need to stretch my legs."

It was obvious that Prouse didn't like hearing that one bit. Even so, he nodded curtly and replied, "Don't go too far."

"I won't."

Lyssa walked up to the bar and studied the place carefully as she went. Compared to scouting out the horizon for miles in every direction while trying to track down a single man, taking in the details of a saloon posed no problem whatsoever.

All it took was one sweep of her eyes and she picked out the other men watching her like hawks. They also stuck out because they were armed and doing a half-assed job of trying to disguise that fact. It was well known that Marshal Earp wasn't too keen on being armed within the town, so that fact alone was enough to separate the locals from the strangers.

By the time she got to the bar and placed her hands down upon the splintered wooden surface, she knew as much as she could know about that bar and its inhabitants. Lyssa smiled, pretended to have stepped in something unpleasant, and then shuffled a few steps over to the left.

When she stopped, she was standing a foot or so away from another woman, who obviously worked there. Judging by the extravagant way her wavy blond hair flowed over her shoulders and was draped onto an expensive red silk dress, her job wasn't serving drinks.

"Help ya, miss?" the barkeep asked.

"I'll take a water in a clean glass." When the barkeep squinted at the way she framed her order, she flicked her eyes toward the armed men at the other end of the bar and added, "It's all right if you need some time to scrounge one up."

Although the barkeep might not have been familiar with the exact situation, he recognized the fact that she wanted some time away from the menacing fellows inhabiting the saloon. "Sure enough," he said. "Just let me know if I take too long."

"Will do. Thanks." Without letting her eyes stray too far

from where she'd been looking before, Lyssa shifted a bit to her left and lowered her voice to a whisper. "Hello there."

The working girl glanced over toward her and sized her up almost as quickly as Lyssa had sized up the entire room. "Hello," she said offhandedly before turning to face the front door again.

"Looking for a customer?"

This time, the blonde looked Lyssa over even more carefully. Her eyes were critical, and a disbelieving smile brought her soft, pink lips to a curl. "I'm flattered, but I stick to the more traditional clients."

"Not me. Him."

Although she looked a bit annoyed, the blonde turned to look where Lyssa had pointed. When she got a look at Prouse seated there, she waved as the man flashed a wary smile.

"He a friend of yours?" the blonde asked.

"Not hardly. Do you know him?"

The working girl sensed the discomfort Lyssa felt at keeping Prouse in her sights for too long. Either that, or she was feeling it herself, because she turned to face the door again. "I've had some words with him, but he wasn't too accommodating."

"Tough customer, huh?"

"You could say that. The men he rides with are good for some quick money, though. I try to stay away from the ones who seem like trouble."

Lyssa snickered and asked, "You think he's too much for you to handle?"

"No, but his friend at the other end of the bar has mean eyes. He tried to take me upstairs, but I wouldn't have any of it. He just looks like he wants to beat on a girl rather than screw her."

Hearing those words come from such a pretty face struck Lyssa as funny. When she laughed, the working girl started laughing as well. They only stopped when the barkeep stepped up to Lyssa's spot.

"Got the glass, but I'm having some water brought in," he said. "That all right?"

"I guess so," Lyssa said in a loud, slightly annoyed voice. She then turned to look at Prouse so she could shrug and shake her head.

Although he wasn't happy about it, Prouse nodded and settled back into his seat.

"Yep," the blonde said. "A real winner. Just like I figured." With a gentle nod, she said, "My name's Brittany."

"I'm Lyssa."

"What's the situation here, Lyssa?"

"I need someone to occupy the time of that man there so I can slip out of this place."

"There's the front door," Brittany said. "Use it."

"I don't think the rest of these gunmen would like that too much."

"Ahh. I see." Grinning, Brittany stepped up close and threaded her arm around Lyssa's. With a smile and a strut that could have melted iron, she said, "Let's turn some heads."

THIRTY-TWO

As she walked beside Brittany, Lyssa couldn't help but take on some of the working girl's swagger. They were surrounded with the swoosh of fine silk as the blonde kicked out her skirts with every step.

"There's a room upstairs with a window that opens onto an alley," Brittany said without effecting her smile. "When you get the chance, slip out and climb down to the street. I've used it plenty of times. It'll hold."

"What do you have in mind here?" Lyssa asked warily.

"Just follow my lead and you'll get your chance. If you find a better way to pull this off, just excuse yourself from the room. I know plenty of ways to make a man let go."

"Thanks," Lyssa said as she was tugged toward the table where Prouse was waiting. "I don't know how to repay you."

But Brittany's eyes were already fixed on Prouse as she whispered, "I'll find a way to make this worth my while."

By this time, they were at Prouse's table. The man sitting there was unable to maintain his cordial smile as his face was overtaken by a mix of confusion and arousal. "What's this about?" he asked.

Already Lyssa could see armed men working their way in closer to the table. They weren't making a big show of force, but they were getting close enough to pounce at a moment's notice.

Brittany, on the other hand, didn't appear to notice anything to put her on her guard. "I heard this pretty lady ordering a water and I couldn't bear it," she said in a breezy voice. "Fine ladies like ourselves deserve wine and nothing less."

One of the bigger gunmen stepped forward and took hold of Brittany by the wrist. "Come along," he snarled. "We ain't interested."

Although she pouted at the way the gunman grabbed her wrist, Brittany didn't move from her spot. "But I thought the three of us could have some fun." Locking eyes with Prouse, she asked, "Isn't that right, Lyssa?"

It wasn't difficult to see how Brittany intended on taking Prouse's mind away from the task at hand. Without missing a beat, she tightened her grip around Brittany's arm and said, "It was a thought."

Prouse flicked his eyes between the two women as if he couldn't believe what he was hearing. "Where the hell did this come from?"

Lyssa shrugged. "I was waiting for my drink, we got to talking, the notion came up . . . and I thought it sounded interesting."

"And what about the matters we were discussing?" Prouse asked.

Lyssa shrugged again, as if that was the only thing she wanted to do at the moment. "I don't feel like talking. At least, not until I've relaxed a little bit. Besides, there's nothing going on around here for at least another day or two." The moment she said that, Lyssa winced and held a hand up to her mouth. "I mean . . . we've got plenty of time to have some fun."

Grinning like a general who'd seen an enemy's army march straight into a trap, Prouse let out a breath and waved away the gunman who'd been closing in on the women. "Why don't you give us some breathing room? If the lady says there's time to talk, than there's time to talk."

Rather than step back immediately, the gunman turned and looked over his shoulder.

Prouse leaned to the side and saw where Hobbes was watching the whole thing from afar. Glaring across the room, he said, "I told you to step back. That should be plenty good enough for you."

After another second, Hobbes nodded. Only then did the gunman let go of Brittany and step back.

"Ah," Brittany said. "That's better. Of course, if you'd like him to come along, I'm sure we could—"

"No, no," Prouse interrupted. "I'd rather have you to myself." He stood up and placed one arm around Brittany's shoulders. He then lowered a tentative arm around Lyssa. When he saw he wasn't about to be pushed away, Prouse grinned and let out a shaky breath. "To be honest, I never even thought of you in this way."

"Don't be shy," Brittany said. "A woman knows when she's being admired by a man. It doesn't matter whether you're standing there or acting bold."

"It doesn't even matter if you're talking about business," Lyssa added. "We just know."

"Really?" Prouse sputtered. "I still don't know if I should—"

Brittany huddled in close to him and rubbed her hand against his chest. "Don't get me all worked up unless you mean to deliver."

Prouse looked over to Lyssa and saw her wink in return. Although he still didn't seem to understand why he was being blessed in such a way, his overpowering instinct was to consider himself a lucky bastard and roll with it as far as he could.

"Where the hell is he going?" Hobbes asked once the gunman came back to the bar.

The gunman was the same one who'd had a grip on Brittany's arm only moments ago. As he stepped over to where Hobbes was waiting, the younger man had a hard time containing his own grin. "Him and them two ladies are going up to a room, by the looks of it."

"That whore's been pestering us since we came to town."

"Yeah, well, it seems like she's convinced that lady into something."

Hobbes watched as Prouse, Brittany and Lyssa all made their way to the stairs. "See what I mean about that dumb shit? We're in the middle of a situation here and he decides to take a few minutes to get his tallywhacker polished."

"That dark-haired one said there wasn't anything happening for another day or two."

"You heard her say that?"

The gunman nodded. "Looks like it slipped out on account of her being in a hurry to get upstairs."

"Then maybe she's just as eager to get under that whore's skirts as Prouse is. Maybe when they're done, we'll all take our turn. No reason we can't have our fun before we kill that bitch." Hobbes watched as the trio went upstairs. "Just keep your eyes and ears open. If she tries to slip out of there, shoot her."

THIRTY-THREE

Somehow, Brittany had managed to slip almost all the way out of the top portion of her dress by the time she reached the door to room number two on the saloon's second floor. Lyssa hadn't seen the blonde pull anything off or even unfasten a single button. Even so, the top of Brittany's dress was wide open and off of both shoulders.

Her pert breasts swayed as she walked and Brittany giggled as if she'd polished off an entire bottle of champagne while going up the stairs. Blond hair flowed over her smooth shoulders, and with one little twitch, one little pink nipple was exposed.

"Oops," Brittany said. "How clumsy of me."

If Prouse had been trying to keep his wits about him, he failed miserably the moment Brittany stumbled forward and gave him that brief little peek. His eyes were wide and he wasn't quite able to answer as he watched her slowly pull her dress up over her breast.

"Umm, don't worry about it," Prouse said once she'd covered herself a bit. "Is Lyssa still with us?"

"I'm right here," Lyssa said as she snapped her eyes away from the neighboring door and put on a quick, flirtatious smile.

Brittany winked and bent at the waist to pull up her skirts and reveal a long, shapely leg. After showing enough bare skin to put a smile onto Prouse's face, she plucked the key that was kept under her garter belt and slipped it into the lock of the door.

"Go right inside," she said while opening the door and ushering Prouse ahead of her. With her free hand, she deftly slipped a second key into Lyssa's hand.

Lyssa took the key, but wasn't able to get over to the door before Prouse stuck his head outside.

"You coming?" he asked eagerly.

Lyssa nodded and stuck the key into her pocket. "Wouldn't miss it for the world."

"Good, good," Prouse said, as if he still couldn't believe how his luck had turned. Just to make certain that luck wasn't about to change right away, he reached out and grabbed Lyssa's hand to pull her inside.

"I wasn't expecting this," Prouse said as he shut the door and immediately began unbuttoning his shirt, "but I sure am looking forward to it."

"Me too," Brittany said as she stepped in front of Prouse and took over in undressing him. While she pulled open the rest of Prouse's shirt, she moved her hands lower so she could unbuckle his pants. All the while, she moved him toward the bed, while also keeping herself in between him and Lyssa.

Straightening her back as much as she could, Brittany peeled off the rest of her dress and slipped it down to reveal her firm little breasts. Unlike the peek she'd given before, Brittany stood tall and arched her back a bit to proudly display her tight curves.

With just a few well-timed wriggles, she got the dress over her hips so it could fall to the floor. All she wore beneath her skirts was a pair of loose-fitting silk underpants. They were trimmed in lace and cut in a way to perfectly accent the shapely round curves of her hips and backside. Even Lyssa found herself admiring Brittany's form.

"You like what you see as much as I do?" Prouse asked as he caught Lyssa staring.

Although she was a little embarrassed to have been caught looking at the other woman, Lyssa put on a smile and nodded a bit. Even though she wouldn't have guessed it, that was the best thing she could have done. Only now did Prouse seem to buy into the fact that all of this was really happening.

Why it was happening no longer mattered to him.

"You two can look all you want," Brittany purred. "I'm sick of waiting." With that, she pulled down Prouse's pants and took hold of his stiff penis. She worked it between her fingers while cupping him with her other hand. She smiled as she saw Prouse's eyes roll up into his head and the rest of him start to waver upon unsteady legs.

All it took was another gentle nudge or two for Brittany to get him over to the narrow bed, which took up a good portion of the room, and then one more to drop him onto the mattress. Prouse landed with a throaty laugh, which turned into a moan as Brittany's lips closed around his cock.

She worked her mouth up and down along his length while also running her tongue against him. Her hands slid up and down against his stomach before working their way up to his chest. Prouse squirmed every now and then, but was unable to speak as Brittany quickened her pace.

Slowly sliding him out of her mouth, Brittany crawled on top of Prouse.

"Wh-where's the other one?" he asked.

Brittany didn't take her eyes off of him as she shrugged, slid off her underpants and said, "Behind me. I think she's a little shy. Besides, she likes to watch me."

"Watch you?"

She nodded and curled her fingers around his cock so she could guide it between her legs. After finding just the right spot, she eased herself down and took him inside of her. "Watch this, baby," Brittany said over her shoulder as she began rocking back and forth.

Prouse could feel his heart slamming in his chest as Brittany rode his cock. Her blond hair was already tousled and flowing over both shoulders. The ends were just long enough to tickle her hard nipples as she glided up and down on his rigid penis.

Prouse reached up to place his hands on her breasts. The moment he got them in his grasp, Brittany clasped her hands on top of his and bounced up and down on him even quicker. All the while, she smiled like a little girl enjoying her turn on a rocking horse.

"You like what you see, baby?" Brittany called out over her shoulder while wriggling her backside.

There was no reply, but Prouse was too preoccupied to notice.

THIRTY-FOUR

Every creak of the boards beneath Lyssa's feet made her certain that she would be discovered. Every crackle in her knees or crunch of her boots against the floor sounded like a clap of thunder in her ears. It seemed like she was moving through molasses, and her heart had already jumped into the back of her throat.

All of that had happened before she'd managed to get out of Brittany's room.

When she'd pushed open the door, she was absolutely certain Prouse would notice. As she crouched down and slipped outside, Lyssa waited to hear the gunshot that would end her life.

But that gunshot didn't come.

The only sound she could hear for those first few moments, apart from the noises she made, was the wheezing and grunting coming from Brittany and Prouse themselves.

Although she did feel a pang of victory in the pit of her stomach, the feeling only lasted for a second. After that, she realized she still had a saloon full of gunmen to contend with. In fact, one of those gunmen was walking no more than ten feet from her at that very second.

Fortunately, he was walking in the opposite direction.

The upper floor of the saloon was open and looked down upon the rest of the main room. Wooden, waist-high rails surrounded the open area, but didn't seem to offer her too much in the way of protection. As Lyssa shuffled the short distance to the neighboring room, she swore that everyone below was looking up at her.

The gunman walking nearby practically came to a stop and was surely going to turn around and spot her at any moment.

Rather than let herself be consumed by those fears, she forced herself to keep moving toward the door until she was close enough to unlock it. Somehow, she got there in one piece. Now all she had to do was fit the key into the lock and get inside.

"Come on over here, darlin'," Prouse said as he draped one hand over Brittany's naked thigh and beckoned with his other.

Still riding him slowly, Brittany glanced back toward the door and then looked back to him with a smile. "She's shy, but she's still enjoying herself."

"Mmmm. I think I want to see that," Prouse replied as he began pushing Brittany to one side and straining to get a clear look around her. Before Prouse could see that he and Brittany were actually the only ones in that room, his view was once again blocked by the blonde's naked body.

Brittany crawled up onto him and straddled his chest. "You just worry about me right now," she scolded. "Don't you want to please this woman before you move on to the next?"

"Sure I do."

"I knew it." Before another word could be spoken, Brittany shifted herself around so she was facing his feet. She then crawled backward and wriggled her wet pussy over Prouse's face. "Want some candy?" she asked.

Prouse got only a fleeting glimpse of the room before Brittany lowered herself down so the downy hair between her legs lightly tickled his nose. The lips of her pussy were slick and pink. When he merely brushed his mouth against them, he could feel Brittany tremble with delight while letting out a giddy squeal.

"Oh my Lord, you're good at that," she groaned.

Prouse took a few tentative licks, which were all treated as if he were the master of all he surveyed. Because he couldn't see much past Brittany's thighs, he was caught completely off guard when he felt her mouth slide all the way down along the length of his cock.

From then on, when he kissed or licked her, he could feel Brittany's moans vibrating all along his penis.

After taking every bit of him into her mouth, Brittany slid her lips up again and listened for any trace of trouble outside. As far as she could tell, there wasn't much of anything going on out there. Then again, it wasn't easy to hear much over the sound of Prouse's growing moans.

Suddenly, Brittany's eyes shot open as Prouse found a particularly sweet spot inside of her with his tongue. Her back arched and she let out the first genuine moan she'd had all day.

"Oh," she groaned. "Do that again."

Prouse grabbed onto her legs and plunged his tongue eagerly into her. She tasted good and he didn't mind going in for seconds. Just as he was about to use his fingers on her, he heard a series of stomping footsteps thundering down the hall.

"What was that?" he asked as he strained to get a look at the door. "Go check on that," he commanded the woman he still thought was watching from another corner of the room. When he didn't get an answer right away, he tried even harder to spot Lyssa. "Hey! You hear me?"

Brittany slid her hands between Prouse's legs and sucked on him as she slid her mouth all the way up again. Just as she'd expected, the move took the breath right out of Prouse's lungs.

"I hear you," she said. "But you're not done with me yet." Without giving him a chance to respond, Brittany scooted down along his chest so she could mount him while keeping her back to him. His rigid cock slipped easily into her and she impaled herself on it while tossing her hair over her shoulder.

Grabbing onto his knees, Brittany straightened her back and glided straight up and down along the length of his erection.

"I thought . . . I thought I heard . . ." Prouse wheezed as Brittany expertly straddled him.

Brittany let out a throaty moan which was just high enough to cover the sound of footsteps thumping toward the door. Just when she heard one set of steps stop in front of the door, she slid her hand down to rub against the tender skin of her clitoris. That, combined with the motion of her hips and the cock inside of her brought a loud groan out of her which filled the room.

Slowly, the footsteps moved along.

Prouse lost his previous train of thought.

Brittany just hoped that Lyssa was all right.

THIRTY-FIVE

Lyssa had thought she was in the clear.

Of course, that was usually when things went to hell.

She'd gotten the key in the lock, turned it and even opened the door a crack without making so much as a sound. When she'd pushed it open and started moving inside, the creak of a rusted hinge grated like a sick cat's meow in her ears.

Since the door was open, she couldn't get a look down the hall at that one gunman who'd been making his rounds. Lyssa's only alternative was to get inside the room and try to lock the door behind her. That's exactly what she did.

That's exactly when she realized that other room wasn't empty.

"Who the hell are you?" a gray-haired man snarled while reaching for his gun.

Lyssa reacted out of pure instinct. She sprung forward using both legs, while reaching out with both hands. Her first impulse was not to use her gun, simply because that would have made too much noise. Of course, a gun would have come in real handy, since the man in that room outweighed her by a good sixty pounds.

With the sounds coming from next door, of squeaking

bedsprings and a headboard knocking against the wall, Lyssa and the man inside that room locked up like a couple of rams fighting over territory. Lyssa grabbed onto the first thing she could, which happened to be the man's face. When she felt him start to push her away, she slammed her leg as close to his groin as she could manage.

Her knee bounced off his thigh, but rattled against an area sensitive enough for him to back off. Once the first wave of pain had passed through him, the man gritted his teeth and came after her with a freshly stoked fire in his eyes.

The man didn't even feel the punch that Lyssa threw at him. Instead, he came straight at her and backhanded her across the cheek. Lyssa reeled back and felt herself tripping over her own feet. She backpedaled to the door, which hadn't been closed all the way. When her shoulders knocked against it, the door flew open and she stumbled out to the railing at the edge of the second floor.

Lyssa spread both arms out to maintain her balance. Once she righted herself, she looked over to see the man inside the room stalking toward her. He was feeling the pain from her first kick with every step, but unfortunately, the men charging toward her from the other end of that floor showed no signs of slowing down.

Even though it felt like she was barely moving, Lyssa bolted into that room like a flicker of lightning. She kicked the door shut with one foot while clasping her hands together and burying them into the gut of the gray-haired man already inside the room. As soon as that man doubled over, she pushed him to the floor and stomped him in the face.

That was more than enough to put him to sleep for a while.

As the men outside the room rushed toward the door, they stopped and gathered in the hall. Lyssa didn't know what they were talking about, but she could hear them discussing something in a series of fierce whispers.

Soon, they began moving again. By the sound of it, they were spreading out to cover her door as well as a few of the others. Deciding not to wait around for them to make their move, Lyssa went to the window that Brittany had told her about and unhooked its latch. The window swung open easily and Lyssa stuck her head outside.

When she saw the sturdy awning directly beneath her, she let out a relieved breath.

"Which door did she go in?" the young man asked. Along with the others on the second floor, he was carrying a gun in his hand and staring at the two doors in front of him.

"How the hell should I know?" another man asked. "I know Mr. Prouse is in one of these rooms."

"Which one?"

Shrugging, the second man knocked on the door and got ready to catch all sorts of hell if he was correct. Instead of hearing Prouse scream at him through the door, he heard another sort of screaming.

Both gunmen glanced at each other and smirked as they heard Brittany moaning loudly in ecstasy.

"Guess that can't be the one," the first gunman whispered.

The second gunman had already moved to the next door. By this time, Hobbes had made it up the stairs and was stalking toward them.

"What the fuck is going on up here?" Hobbes snarled.

"That woman Mr. Prouse was talking to was up here wandering around. At least, I'm pretty sure it was her. I only got a quick look."

"Where's Prouse?"

Both gunmen paused before nodding toward the first door. Before Hobbes could ask what Prouse was doing in there, he got his answer in the form of another throaty moan from Brittany.

"He's in there with that whore?" Hobbes asked in disbelief.

"Sounds that way."

"Jesus Christ."

"You want us to pull him out of there?"

"Don't bother," Hobbes replied. "At least in there he's not fucking us over. Where did that other bitch go?"

"Got to be in there," the gunman said while pointing toward the next door in the row.

"Then bust it down before I use your goddamn skulls to do the job."

Both gunmen kicked in the door, which was nearly enough to break it off its hinges. When they stepped inside, they found some overturned furniture, an unconscious man and an open window.

THIRTY-SIX

Lyssa crouched and moved as fast as she could along the overhang. Since she didn't want to break her leg, she headed for the lowest part of the roof so she could have an easy drop to the street. Unfortunately, that took her directly past the window of the room where Brittany was keeping Prouse occupied.

As she crept toward that window, she could hear commotion coming from the room she'd just left behind. Lyssa felt the urge to run like a fire burning in her belly. Steeling herself for the worst, she hunkered down and made a straight line for the edge of the overhang.

"I . . . hear something," Prouse said as Brittany bucked and wriggled on top of him.

She was straddling his hips and riding his cock like she was on top of a bucking bronco. Her hands were pressed against his chest and she pumped her hips up and down in quick, short thrusts. Since she was feeling enough pleasure of her own, she knew that Prouse was knocking on heaven's door. All she had to do to confirm that fact was look at him.

Despite the commotion that was building outside, Prouse had his hands full with Brittany. She climbed all over him, as though she was the one having her way with him. Since she was such a bundle of energy, he'd stopped wondering when Lyssa was going to join in.

Brittany straightened up and dug her fingers through her hair, giving the man beneath her a glorious view of her bare breasts and smooth, heaving belly. One hand worked its way down the front of her body until it could rub her glistening clitoris. While she pleasured herself, rode him and moaned at the same time, Brittany gave Prouse a show no man could resist.

Although Brittany seemed to be staring off into space as she arched her back and pulled in a deep, climactic breath, she was actually focused on the movement happening just outside the window. She could see Lyssa working her way past the other side of the glass and could hear the stomping footsteps that were chasing her.

Until now, Prouse had been fairly easy to distract. At the moment, things were getting too loud to be ignored.

"Hold on," Prouse said as he began to regain his senses. "I think there's something going on."

"You're right about that," Brittany said. "I'm about to lose my breath again."

"No, I . . ."

Even though Brittany was able to stop him in mid-sentence with a creative flick of her finger at the spot where he was entering her, she knew that he would hear the stomping and voices sooner rather than later. Lyssa was almost past the window, but it still seemed as though Prouse was about to look in that direction at any possible moment.

Suddenly, Brittany let out a shuddering moan and her eyes shot open wide. Falling forward as if she no longer had the strength to stay upright, she caught herself at the last moment with both hands against the mattress.

Those hands also managed to be on either side of Prouse's head, which kept him from looking to either side while also pressing against both of his ears. She ignored his attempts to shake free and pressed her hips tightly against

his so that his cock was buried deeper inside of her than it
had ever been before.

Not only was that enough to pull Prouse's attention away
from everything else going on in that saloon, but it rushed
him straight to the brink of his own climax. With Brittany
enveloping him so completely, he could feel her pussy tightening around him. As she trembled with her oncoming orgasm, he could feel every bit of that as well.

Prouse couldn't tell what noises were coming from outside his room and which ones were coming from himself.
His own breathing and heartbeat were a flood of noise inside
his head. As Brittany lowered herself down so her breasts
were pressed against his chest, Prouse's first instinct was to
pump up into her.

After that, the rush of sound coming from the two of
them only got louder.

Brittany was surprised to feel a genuine climax working
its way through her body. Although Prouse wasn't the best
lover she'd ever had, she'd been working hard enough on
him to get herself right up to the brink. She did have to give
him some credit for pushing her over the edge.

Shaking her hair so it fell over Prouse's face, Brittany
took another look outside and saw the last flicker of movement as Lyssa slipped past the window and headed for the
edge of the awning. It was hard to say whether the other
woman was falling or if she'd jumped on her own accord,
but Brittany knew there wasn't anything else she could do to
help. All that remained now was to finish up and see about
tending to business.

Her nipples were still erect from the orgasm that had
pulsed through her body and Prouse was losing strength as if
it was leaking out of him through a hole in his back. His
hands were clamped onto her hips and slowly rubbing the
curve of her backside.

She was still wriggling her hips in a slow, grinding circle
to prolong the pleasure that had already taken a firm hold on
him. Just when his eyes began to refocus, she shifted again

and sat back up while dragging her fingernails over his chest.

"Oh my Lord," he wheezed. "That was amazing."

Brittany eased herself off of him and swung her legs over the side of the bed. Even though the noises within the saloon were louder than ever, she barely noticed them. When she glanced behind her, she saw that Prouse was already drifting off to sleep. With a sly grin, Brittany reached out for the bundle of Prouse's clothes. She found his money after less than two seconds of searching.

THIRTY-SEVEN

The first gunman caught sight of Lyssa and immediately jumped out the window after her. He lost his footing almost instantly and landed heavily on his side. From there, he began skidding toward the edge of the low-hanging roof.

The second gunman was about to jump out as well before Hobbes grabbed him by the shoulder and pulled him back into the room.

"Forget it," Hobbes said as he carefully stepped out the window. "Get downstairs and see if you can find her." Even as he got his footing and moved along the outside of the saloon, he had a real good picture in his mind of what he was going to find.

When Hobbes made it to the edge of the overhang and looked to the street below, he saw that his mental picture wasn't too far off.

Amid a flurry of stomping feet and slamming doors, the gunman ran outside and dashed into the street. He stopped and turned in a quick circle while pointing his pistol at anything that moved. Dumbfounded, he turned his sights higher and quickly spotted Hobbes looking down at him. "I think she got away."

"Really?" Hobbes snarled. "I never would've guessed."

• • •

Lyssa bolted down the street, expecting to be spotted and killed at any moment. Even though she'd been waiting for that same thing for a while now, the sensation still cut through her like a blade slicing through smooth skin.

The streets were coming more alive and there wasn't a friendly face to be seen. Since the marshal and his deputies were scattered and doing different tasks, a badge was awfully scarce right about then. But it wasn't a badge that gave her a sudden burst of hope. It wasn't even a familiar face picking her out of the crowd.

It was a horse.

To be more precise, it was a black Darley Arabian stallion that caught her eye and got her running with her arms waving wildly over her head.

The stallion was moving at a good pace and the man in the saddle was staring intently forward. At first, it seemed as if they were going to run straight past her. But when he spotted her, the rider pulled back on the reins and brought the horse to a stop.

"Lyssa?" Clint asked. "Is that you?"

Before she could get a word out, Lyssa ran up to him and held up her arm. The moment Clint took her hand, she pulled herself up and into the saddle behind him. "Get out of here," she gasped. "Just go."

Clint steered Eclipse toward a side street and snapped the reins. After riding for a block, he leaned back and asked, "This good enough for you or do I have to leave town?"

"This is good," she replied. "Just stay away from the Rusty Nail."

"Why?"

"Let's just say I wasn't supposed to get out of there alive."

"What happened?" Just as that question left Clint's mouth, he heard a commotion on the street behind him. Turning to look over his shoulder, he spotted a group of men running into the intersection he'd just used, so they could stop and look in every direction.

"Let me guess," Clint said. "Those are the men you were running from."

"You got it."

"Did Prouse approach you after we split up?"

"Not him, but one of the men working for him." While she was trying to catch her breath, Lyssa started to laugh. "Prouse came at me later and I got to say that he took me by surprise."

Clint pointed Eclipse in the opposite direction as the men at the corner and rode casually away from them. "He didn't try to take a shot at you right away, did he?"

"No. Better than that. He got dressed up in a fancy suit and tried to convince me he was a lawyer or something."

"What?"

Lyssa was laughing harder by now and had her arms wrapped around Clint's waist so she could rest against his back. "He tried to weasel some information out of me, and it might have worked a bit if I hadn't known from the start he was full of shit."

"Did you manage to find out anything for yourself?"

"A bit. How about you?"

Clint nodded. "And we've got to tell Virgil all about it before this turns into another one of his infamous dustups."

THIRTY-EIGHT

When Clint and Lyssa got back to Virgil's office, they were just in time to find the marshal and his deputies unlocking the long, narrow cupboard where they locked up their guns. While a couple of the younger lawmen reflexively twitched toward their holsters, Virgil gave the new arrivals a quick sideways glance.

"Where've you been?" Virgil asked.

"I went to scout out that camp," Clint said.

"Not you," Virgil said as he nodded toward Lyssa. "I meant her."

She shrugged and replied, "I've been doing some scouting of my own."

Gripping a shotgun in his good hand, Virgil stomped over to her until he was less than one pace away and bearing down on her. His posture was even imposing to the ones who weren't standing directly in front of it. "You want to work for me, then you don't go charging off like some angry god-damn kid."

"Virgil," Clint cut in, "there's something you should—"

"Just a minute," Virgil snapped without taking his eyes off of Lyssa. "This is between me and her. You know how I operate, Lyssa. We've worked together plenty of times. I

157

wanted you to be in on this, but you know damn well you need to go about it properly."

Lyssa held her ground. In fact, she even straightened up a bit so she could meet Virgil's glare as straight-on as she could. "Yeah, Marshal. I know all about how you operate. That's why me and Clint knew we had to do it our own way."

Now Virgil's eyes shifted in their sockets so he could spread his ire between both Clint and Lyssa. "What?"

"It was my idea as much as it was hers," Clint said. "We needed someone to get close to those killers, and she's the only one who could have passed as someone who hadn't seen Prouse's face yet."

"But she's seen him plenty of times," Virgil muttered.

Clint smirked and replied, "But they don't know that. It's like you told me . . . she's one of the best."

Virgil nodded, but still didn't look too happy about what he was hearing. "Keep talking."

"I got real close to him," Lyssa explained. "They bought into the whole act of me and Clint parting on such bad terms. That's when they came to me and tried to get me to spill some information."

"What kind of information?"

"Like what was going to happen to that prisoner, when he might be tried, that sort of thing."

"They wanted his whole schedule," Virgil said, more as a way to voice his own thoughts.

Lyssa nodded. "Pretty much. Seems like they wanted to find out where you and all your deputies might be in the near future. At least, that's how I took it."

"Me too," Clint said.

Virgil sided with them by easing up a bit from Lyssa and nodding as well. "You could have come to me with this."

"They might have seen you two putting your heads together," Clint said. "Even if they didn't, you wouldn't let her walk in there on her own like that. Hell, you insisted on deputizing me. That sort of thing would have gotten her shot before she got half as close to Prouse as she did."

"Maybe," Virgil said while shifting a disapproving glare in Clint's direction. "But she would have been a hell of a lot safer."

"She knew the risks," Clint told him. "The most dangerous stuff was her idea. Since we needed to act quickly, I let her do things her own way. You've got to admit she's been handling herself well enough to have earned that trust. Besides, we're all in danger here."

Although Virgil clearly understood what Clint was saying, he simply wasn't the sort of man to say as much out loud. Instead, he let out a sigh and asked, "Does this all have to do with the commotion outside the Rusty Nail?"

"More or less," Clint replied.

Virgil nodded and relaxed a bit. After a wave from him, the deputies eased up a bit as well. "What about you, Clint? What happened at that camp?"

Clint's breath caught in the back of his throat. "Didn't Michael make it back here to tell you?"

"He did, but he was bleeding pretty bad. He was getting patched up, and he passed out before he could say much."

After letting out the breath he'd been holding, Clint replied, "We found the camp along with a good amount of hired guns."

"And they were with Prouse?"

Clint nodded. "They were waiting for a signal and then they meant to split up, ride into town from different sides and kill as many as they could in the crossfire."

"That's pretty specific," Virgil mused. "You sure about all that?"

As Clint thought back to the terrorized look on that last gunman's face, he said, "Yeah. I'm sure."

"Michael did say there weren't many left breathing at that camp."

"True enough. There may be one or two, but the rest didn't leave us much choice."

Virgil nodded and walked over to his office's window. "No need for explanation. You're a duly appointed enforcer of the law here in Colton. Unlike some folks I might mention."

This time, Lyssa was the one to let out the prolonged and aggravated sigh. "Fine, just pin the badge on me and be done with it. I can't exactly waltz back into that saloon and fool anyone anymore."

Glancing over to Cole, Virgil motioned for the deputy to get another badge. After going through the motions of swearing her in, Virgil said, "One last thing. Was that spat you two had in the restaurant even real?"

"No."

"Then what did Clint whisper into your ear to get you to slap him like that?"

"Simple," she said with a shrug. "He told me to slap him and make it count."

Shaking his head, Virgil looked over to Clint. "I guess Wyatt's right. Sometimes I do tend to overthink things."

THIRTY-NINE

Hobbes stormed into the Rusty Nail after leading the charge into the street. Since he was only coming back with the same men that had followed him out, he wasn't in the best of moods. In fact, his bellowing voice and all the weapons being drawn had cleared out the saloon of everyone but Prouse, his men and a few hardened employees.

Brittany was one of the latter, and she ducked into another room with triple her normal fee stuffed between her breasts. Prouse came out with his clothes rumpled and badly buttoned. His holster was around his waist, and he drew his gun the moment he crossed the threshold of the upstairs room.

"Finally seeing fit to join the rest of us?" Hobbes snarled.

Prouse was still looking around while using his free hand to tuck in his shirt. "Where is she?"

"Good fucking question. Last I saw that bitch, she was jumping down from the roof outside your window."

"Not her," Prouse said with a vicious sneer. "The whore who was in there with me. She stole my goddamn money!"

Hobbes stared openmouthed at Prouse for a solid couple of seconds. Since everyone else inside that saloon was

161

watching the two of them, it seemed more like a solid couple of hours.

Slowly, Hobbes walked over to Prouse, pulled back an arm and backhanded the other man so hard that he knocked Prouse against the door frame. Even though Prouse wheeled around as if to challenge Hobbes, he knew better than to follow through.

"All you're worried about is some pocket money?" Hobbes asked. "The bitch that crawled out that window knows how many of us are here and is probably talking to the marshal right now!"

"I'm not the one wasting time throwing punches!"

"No," Hobbes shot back. "You're the one wasting time dressing up like a fool and fucking some whore."

"They were both supposed to be—" But Prouse stopped in the middle of his attempted explanation when he saw the bloody promise in Hobbes's eyes. After realizing there was no real way to regain his pride without taking his own life in his hands, Prouse sucked it up and straightened his shirt. "I thought she was in there with me."

"Whatever you thought, it don't matter no more. Did you mention anything about busting Bill out of jail?"

"No," Prouse said sharply.

"Did you mention anything about him or the jail?"

"That's what I was trying to find out, wasn't I? How could I avoid asking anything about that?"

"And that's exactly why I wanted to snatch her, drag her into a room and start cutting things off of her until she talked. Even if she didn't say a damn thing, we'd at least still have a hostage! Everyone knows Marshal Earp wouldn't make a move against us if he thought we'd kill a hostage. Especially someone he's already sweet on."

The longer he stood there, the more Prouse resembled a mouse that had been flushed out of its hole and had no clue where it was or what it should do. Once the last shred of fight had gone out of him, he lowered his head and leaned back against the wall. "So what do we do now?"

While Prouse may have looked pathetic, Hobbes took on a distinctly different appearance. His eyes narrowed into angry slits and focused upon Prouse alone. His mouth formed into a thin line as he moved forward with such quickness that he seemed to just disappear from one spot and then reappear in another.

Standing so close to Prouse that his breath washed over the other man's face, Hobbes snarled, "We agreed you'd play the leader on this so I could keep out of sight. You'd best act the part while all these men are watching or I'll have to step in and show them who's really calling the shots."

"I've got every bit as much reason to want those Earps dead as you do," Prouse squeaked.

When Hobbes responded to that, his lips barely moved. It looked more like a voice was coming from the side of a slab of granite. "You knew some of those assholes that were killed in Tombstone because they hired you for a few odd jobs. I lost blood relatives once those pimps started seeking out their vengeance.

"I was willing to look the other way after that street fight, because it was a fight that needed to happen just to clear the air. But once those Earps started hunting down men like they were animals, that's where I draw the line. So don't stand there and tell me we're in the same boat. You lost a few acquaintances. I lost kin."

Prouse gulped and nodded. "I know."

"Then stop acting like the big dog around here and do what we came to do. If you want to waste time dipping your wick, then tell me right now and I'll be glad to part ways."

Prouse glanced down at Hobbes's hand to find it drifting closer to his holster. That hand was steady as a rock and waited over the pistol at his side like a well-trained dog waiting for the command to attack.

"I . . . made a mistake," Prouse admitted in a voice that was only slightly louder than a whisper. "I'm sorry."

"What was that?"

Knowing what Hobbes was after, Prouse swallowed what

remained of his pride and raised his voice so all the men looking on could hear. "I said I was sorry."

That seemed to be enough to satisfy Hobbes for the moment. Although he wasn't exactly grinning, he did move his hand away from his gun and take a step back. "All right," he said. "Now let's get Bill out of that jail cell."

"We're still going after him?"

"Hell yes, we are. This party might have gotten started a little quicker than we thought, but it's still gonna happen."

FORTY

"They're coming," Virgil said. "I can feel it."

Clint, Lyssa and the other deputies had already cleaned out the gun cabinets and were in the process of getting every last firearm ready to use when those grim words came out of the marshal's mouth.

Clint's reflex was to look outside rather than question Virgil's instincts. "You think they'll try hitting us here or at the jail?"

"I think they intend on hitting both at the same time. Then again," Virgil added with a grin, "we know that ain't gonna happen."

"Not if they're counting on backup from those men camped outside of town."

"Are there any more camps we should be worried about?"

Clint shook his head. "That was the only one. I was very thorough when I asked about that."

As a show of mutual respect, Virgil wasn't about to question Clint's instinct on that matter. "Good. Now all we need to do is guess which place they intended on hitting with which group of men."

"I'd say your best bet is to watch the jail," Lyssa said.

Virgil looked over to her and asked, "Why there over this office?"

"Because they intend on breaking out the prisoner held there."

"Did anyone mention why they're so intent on getting that man back? As far as any of us know, he was just a scout."

"I don't know much about him," Lyssa replied, "but I do know they were asking a lot of questions as to when he would stand trial, where he was being held, when he would be moved and all that. Also, since they obviously didn't figure on me getting out of that saloon to tell you about it, I don't see any reason for them to cover their intentions."

"Their intentions are to kill me," Virgil said without much of any emotion in his voice. "There's no question about that."

"Will they still follow through on that or will they just try to collect their man and get out of here to try some other time?" Clint asked.

"They won't go anywhere."

"You sound awfully sure of that, Virgil."

"I am." Virgil pulled in a breath and leaned against the wall next to the front window. He winced and rubbed his bad arm while watching the street through the glass. "One of the men Lyssa described inside the Rusty Nail is named Hobbes. He'll want to come after me no matter what the cost."

"Any particular reason?" Clint asked.

"Sure. Me and Wyatt killed three of his cousins."

"When did this happen?"

"It was after I got out of Tombstone. I was living in Prescott and hoping to God Wyatt wasn't getting himself killed. He turned up on my doorstep one day and said he found two of the men who'd taken the shot at me that . . ." As Virgil trailed off, he nodded toward his left side and the arm that hung limply from that shoulder. Rather than finish his sentence, he looked up and skipped ahead.

"I'd been calling Wyatt a hypocrite for chasing after vengeance and calling it justice, but after losing Morgan and part of me as well, Wyatt's offer to ride along with him for once sounded pretty good." Virgil lowered his eyes and his voice as if he was the only one in the room. "It was stupid. I know that. Hell, I knew it back then. But those bastards couldn't just ride off after what they'd done. That's not justice and it just ain't right.

"I rode out with Wyatt, met up with Doc, and we found those dogs hiding in a run-down old ranch. I recognized them right away from the night I was shot. Every damn moment from that night was burned into my eyes, and when I saw them again, I wanted to burn them down where they stood.

"Turns out we didn't have to make a choice in the matter, since they recognized us as well and started shooting. It was chaos and bloody as hell, but at least it was over quick. Those assholes couldn't fight for shit when my back wasn't turned and we left them in the dirt where they belonged. One of them was named Rupert Hobbes. Over the last few months, I've heard of another Hobbes trying to track me down. Sometimes, I think I should just let him find me and be done with it. I'm sick of all this fighting over old wounds."

Clint stepped up to Virgil and put a hand on the older man's shoulder. "Whatever your intentions were, it sounds like you three did the same job any official posse would have done."

"That is if I remember it right," Virgil said. "Or if folks believe a damn word I say on the subject."

"I believe you," Clint said. "Things like this aren't the sort of things a man can forget . . . even if he wants to. As for anyone else, it doesn't much matter what they think on the subject."

"No," Virgil said grimly. "I suppose it doesn't."

"This does answer our question, though," Clint said.

Virgil nodded. "Hobbes will be coming after me. Even if he sends some men to the jail, he'll be coming for me."

"Right. We also know he'll be shorthanded."

"Did you find out what the signal was to be that was supposed to call in those reinforcements?"

Reluctantly, Clint said, "No."

"All the same, the important thing is that this thing will be over soon. For better or worse, all these loose ends will be tied up."

"It'll be for the better," Clint said. "That's what I'm here for."

Virgil's brushy mustache curled up a bit at the edges when he heard that. It curled up even more when he saw Lyssa and all the deputies step forward.

"It's what we're all here for," one of the younger lawmen said.

"Well, I do appreciate it. Just do me a favor and watch yourselves out there. These men are a mix of wild and desperate, which never bodes well for anyone."

There were nods all around.

Virgil looked outside and straightened up. "All right, everyone. Look sharp. A few of them just rounded the corner."

FORTY-ONE

Prouse and one other gunman snuck from one alley to another on their way to the jailhouse. They scurried from shadow to shadow as darkness closed in around them. Even though the sunlight seemed to soak into the California sky and stay a bit longer than in most places, the shadows would still claim Colton before too much longer.

Doing his best to watch the folks on the street without meeting any of their eyes, Prouse got to a spot where he could see the front half of the jailhouse. The man next to him settled against the wall and stuck his hands casually into his pockets.

"Where's Danny?" Prouse asked.

"He ain't back yet."

Leaning forward, Prouse stared down the street until he picked out one figure that distinguished itself from the rest. That figure weaved through the other people and headed straight for the jailhouse. It shifted toward Prouse once it got close enough to see him.

Danny was a skinny man in his late teens with a dirty face and gun strapped to his hip that looked heavier than the rest of his body.

"Did you give the signal?" Prouse asked anxiously.

169

Nodding vigorously, Danny said, "I sure did. See for yourself."

Both Prouse and the other man looked toward one end of town. It didn't take much to spot the flicker of light on the horizon. Now that their eyes were becoming even more adjusted to the dark, they could see a billowing trail of smoke as well.

Prouse grinned at the sight of the fire on the roof of the distant building. He didn't seem to care too much about the shouts that were coming from the locals who'd spotted that same blaze.

"It shouldn't be long before them others get here," Prouse said. "There's no way for them to miss that."

The man next to Prouse nodded. "Shouldn't be long before they get here."

"By the time we get into that jail and work our way out again, our own little cavalry will be giving the law a whole new set of headaches."

"How much longer should we wait before heading in?" Danny asked.

"How long's the signal been lit?"

"Fire's been going for fifteen minutes or so."

A bit of the eagerness in Prouse's eyes dimmed, but he did a fair job of maintaining his expression. He even sounded more or less the same when he said, "Let's give it a little while longer. Just to make sure Hobbes gets where he needs to be."

Virgil Earp stepped out of his office, followed by several of his deputies. He was carrying a shotgun in the crook of his arm and had a pistol holstered within easy reach of that same hand. Although he walked with something of a limp and had one arm that was less than useful, he still had an air of strength about him that nobody could deny.

His eyes narrowed as he adjusted to the dark. With a couple sweeping waves of his arm, he got the few curious onlookers to step back and give him some room. Shaking his head, he focused on the street and said, "It never fails to amaze me how many will turn out to see a fight."

Standing on Virgil's left, Lyssa tightened her grip on her rifle. "Can't really blame them. This is bound to be a hell of a show."

Rolling his eyes a bit, Virgil replied, "Just stay back somewhere you can provide some cover. Might as well put that rifle to good use."

"Will do."

Once Lyssa left, the place she'd been standing was filled by another deputy carrying a pistol. Virgil pulled in a breath to steady himself and let it out slowly. By this time, he could make out Hobbes's face and burning eyes settled in the midst of several other gunmen. The entire group walked straight down the middle of the street with their guns in plain sight.

"This looks familiar," Virgil muttered.

One of the younger deputies leaned in a bit. "What was that, Marshal?"

"Nothing. I count four of them. What about you?"

"Six. There's two in the back behind the others."

Virgil squinted and then nodded. "My eyes aren't what they used to be. Six it is."

Hobbes walked down the street and stopped with about ten paces between himself and the lawmen. The hired guns accompanying Hobbes fanned out so every one of them could take a shot at the marshal and his deputies at a moment's notice.

"Surprised to see you out here like this, Virgil," Hobbes said. "I thought it was more your style to bushwhack someone when their back was turned."

"You want to turn your back? I'll be more than happy to knock you over the head and toss you in a cell so you can think this over."

Shaking his head, Hobbes said, "Don't need any of that. I've had plenty of time to think about this. My only regret is that your pimp of a brother ain't here to take his medicine along with you."

"If I were you, I wouldn't hope for Wyatt to show up. He's not as good-natured as I am."

"Yeah, you were real friendly when you busted into my cousin's house with guns blazing."

"Were you there?"

"If I had been, you wouldn't be alive."

"Then don't talk about something you don't know a damn thing about."

It was plain to see by the look on Hobbes's face that he was not used to being talked to like that. Even so, he managed to keep from lashing out the way he would with anyone else.

"You've got one more chance to drop your guns and walk out of here with nothing more than a misdemeanor charged against you. Push this any further and it'll be ugly. I promise you that."

Hobbes shook his head slowly and squared his shoulders. "You can stuff those misdemeanors up your ass," he snarled. "Tonight's the night hell catches up to you."

"All right, then. Have it your way."

FORTY-TWO

Danny was breathless as he ran back to where Prouse and the other gunman were standing. Part of that was because Danny was worked up about the fight that was brewing and part of it was because he'd practically run from one end of town to the other.

"They're not here yet," Danny reported. "But they've got to be here soon."

"We can wait," Prouse said.

"I did see Hobbes and the rest. They're facing down Marshal Earp and those deputies right now."

"You hear that?" the other gunman said as he got a better grip on his shotgun. "We need to get started right now. Those others will get here on time. You know they can ride faster than anyone."

Looking at the expectant faces of the two men, Prouse started to feel like he had when he was accepted as the leader of the entire group. As that confidence returned, he stood up a little straighter and talked with a bit more of an edge to his voice. "You're right. Let's do this."

Both other gunmen smiled widely and nodded. They practically jumped toward the jailhouse the moment Prouse made a move in that direction. The three men were able to

get across the street without attracting a single glance. It
seemed that Danny wasn't the only one who knew about the
confrontation between Hobbes and the marshal.

There was only one deputy posted in front of the jailhouse,
and it was the same one who'd been watching Bill since he
was tossed into his cell. Prouse walked right up to the deputy
and settled his hand on top of his holstered pistol.

"You got a prisoner in there that needs to be set free,"
Prouse said.

Cole didn't look away from his newspaper as he replied,
"Trial's in a bit. That's when it'll be decided if he's to be set
free."

"I told you to let him out," Prouse snapped as he drew his
pistol and aimed it at the deputy. "Right now."

Cole folded his newspaper and dropped it before slowly
getting to his feet. "You sure you want to do this?"

Prouse's expression took on a definite change. Where
he'd been nervous before and more confident recently, he
now looked off-balance. Rather than make another threat, he
sighted along the barrel of his gun and tightened his finger
around the trigger.

A single shot blasted through the air, shattering a window
and then carving a messy tunnel through flesh and bone.
Prouse stumbled back a step as if the floor had tilted beneath
his feet. He gazed at the pistol in his hand with shock. There
was no smoke coming from the barrel, but the shot was still
echoing through the air.

When he looked down to see the blood coming from the
fresh wound in the meaty part of his shoulder, Prouse gasped
and let his gun arm drop. "What . . . what?" was all he could
get out before the pain rushed in on him like a flood.

The other two gunmen were just as shocked as Prouse
when they saw that he was wounded and Cole was still un-
touched. They blinked a few times at the deputy, which gave
Clint just enough time to come out from the jail.

"Sorry about that, Cole," Clint said to the deputy. "I

thought they'd want to get inside and check on their friend before doing anything stupid."

"So long as it turned out all right," Cole replied as he put his back to the jailhouse. "I kind of figured they'd do something stupid the first chance they got."

"My mistake." Still holding the smoking Colt in his hand, Clint locked eyes with the gunmen. "Now let's see how stupid you're willing to get."

With those words still hanging in the air, one of the gunmen steeled himself, lifted his shotgun and took aim.

Clint picked up on the first twitch on that gunman's face, which was enough to tell him the man had already made up his mind. Just to be certain, Clint gave the man a grace period of half a second. That was more than enough to let Clint know the shotgunner was beyond the point of reason.

Keeping his eyes on him, Clint aimed the modified Colt as if he was pointing his finger, and then pulled the trigger. The gun barked once and spat a round through the shotgunner's face, knocking the man over and tossing him directly into the street.

"Watch it!" Cole shouted as he drew his own weapon and pointed it almost directly at Clint.

With all his senses soaking up every last detail, Clint knew better than to worry about Cole. Instead, he pivoted on one foot to clear the deputy's line of fire while also turning to face Prouse straight on.

Clint fired first, with Cole a fraction of a second behind him. Both men hit Prouse just as he'd managed to lift his gun again and take aim. One bullet punched a hole through Prouse's skull and the other nailed him in the chest.

Prouse was killed so quickly that he would show up at the gates of heaven with a stupid, surprised look on his face. He was wearing that very look for the few seconds he remained upright. After that, he fell against the jailhouse and landed in a heap.

Clint and Cole shifted their aim to Danny, who had already turned white as a sheet.

"Your move, boy," Clint said.

"There's others coming," Danny sputtered. "If you know what's good for you, you'll just—"

"I cleared that camp outside of town myself," Clint interrupted. "Nobody's coming from there apart from a few ghosts."

Danny not only lowered his gun, but he also seemed on the verge of pissing himself as he stammered, "I . . . I don't . . . You can . . . just . . ."

Reaching out, Clint took the gun from Danny's hand and promptly turned it on its previous owner. "You got room in there for one more?" he asked Cole.

The deputy leaned into the jailhouse and saw Bill staring out with wide, eager eyes. Once he saw who was still standing, the prisoner cursed under his breath and dropped back onto his cot.

"Yeah," Cole said with relief. "It looks like his friend could use some company."

FORTY-THREE

The street had cleared to the point where it seemed as if the wind had swept in and blown away everyone but Virgil Earp, his deputies, Hobbes and his men. Word had spread like wildfire through Colton, until every window and door was filled with eyes peering out to see how this fight would end.

Judging by the looks of Virgil's and Hobbes's faces, it wouldn't end happily.

As he stood there, Virgil could feel the twitching pain in his old shotgun wound which had become something of a constant companion. It ripped through his back and left side until it felt like the tips of the fingers on his left hand were on fire.

Memories rushed through his head, along with plenty of regrets. But it was too late to worry about those anymore. The die had been cast. All that remained was to deal with it.

Hobbes planted his feet and glared right back at Virgil. The men around him held their ground, knowing they might get shot by Hobbes themselves if they took the first shot at Marshal Earp.

The hate flowed through Hobbes's blood as it had for the last several years. Even though he'd put a name to that hate, it didn't make it burn any less now that he was face-to-face with

177

the man belonging to that name. In fact, the more he stared at Virgil, the hotter Hobbes's blood boiled inside of him.

Soon, however, Hobbes began to shift on his feet. The sounds of gunfire erupted from nearby, followed by the echo of a few familiar voices. And, just as quickly as they had come, those noises faded away. His eyes wanted to look down one of the other streets, and a subtle hint of confusion showed up as a little crease in his brow.

"What's the matter, Hobbes?" Virgil asked. "You expecting more of a distraction?"

The crease in Hobbes's brow deepened a bit.

Virgil nodded, picking up on every one of those signals as if they were painted in large letters across that other man's cheek. "We found those boys you had posted outside of town. I guess you should have kept a closer eye on them."

Even though the nail had been hit firmly upon its head, Hobbes didn't want to give Virgil the satisfaction of telling him as much. That frustration fed into his anger like kindling being chucked into an already roaring flame. When he looked at Virgil and his deputies to find nothing but calm eyes staring back at him, Hobbes couldn't choke down another bit of it.

"I don't need any distractions," Hobbes growled. "And I don't need anyone at my side." With that, he snatched the gun from his side and lifted it to fire. Every one of the men next to Hobbes had been waiting for that very thing and they brought up their guns while tightening fingers around triggers.

Even though he was the only man with only one arm at his disposal, Virgil was the first among the lawmen to take his shot. He grimaced while holding up his bad arm to support his shotgun and steady it as he laid the weapon across the arm and sighted down the barrel. Virgil pulled his trigger and didn't so much as wince at the lead that was being thrown at him.

Although they weren't first to shoot, Virgil's deputies were less than a second late in doing so. A few of them dropped to one knee and a couple dove for cover. One of them stayed put rather than leave Virgil in the street on his own.

Lyssa was out there with Virgil, even though she was one of the bodies to drop down while bringing her gun up to fire. Despite the fact that she wasn't a gunfighter by any stretch of the imagination, she was just too stubborn to admit to that fact.

She fired as quickly as she could pull her trigger. Rather than take the time to aim and steady herself, she just pointed the business end of her pistol at the group of men in front of her and got some bullets flying in that direction.

Two of Hobbes's men were cut down instantly. Although one could have been hit by any number of shooters, one of them was tossed through the air so far that only a shotgun could have done the job.

Those weren't the only casualties within that opening salvo, however. One of Virgil's deputies twitched as if he'd been clipped along a shoulder or leg. When he staggered back, however, he dropped his gun and fell to his knees as blood soaked through the front of his shirt. He flopped face-down into the dirt and died on the spot.

Now that the first shots had been spent, those still in the fight were doing their best to live through the next few seconds. Deputies and gunmen scattered while still firing off rounds. Another clap of thunder issued from Virgil's shotgun to scatter those men like the buckshot that had come from his barrel.

"Get around back," Hobbes snarled to one of his men. "See if you can get behind them and keep them busy for a while longer."

The gunman nodded and ran around the marshal's office. Although he got clear of the crossfire, he nearly ran straight into Clint, who was headed toward the fray.

Although he was surprised by the sudden arrival of the gunman, Clint had enough of his wits about him to keep moving forward and send his forearm straight out and across the other man's upper body. Clint connected at the man's shoulders, just beneath his neck. The impact practically knocked the man out of his boots and sent his back slamming against the ground, to drive all the air from his lungs.

Clint's first impulse was to sight down the Colt's barrel and aim at the gunman's face. But when he saw the man squirm and sputter on the ground while desperately trying to suck in a breath, Clint knew he wasn't about to get much resistance from that one. Rather than shoot the guy, Clint kicked the gun from his hand and sent the butt of his pistol into the gunman's chin.

By this time, another of Hobbes's men had spotted Clint and took a quick shot at him.

Clint heard the hiss of lead screaming past him and reacted out of pure reflex. He bent his gun arm at the elbow, fired a single shot and followed it up with another.

The gunman in the distance twitched and jerked as the bullets hit him, but he still took another shot at Clint. That shot drilled into the ground a few yards shy of where Clint was standing. The man who'd fired it was already on the ground and gasping for breath.

"I got you now, asshole!" Hobbes shouted as he fired his last few rounds at Virgil.

"Give it up before you're dead," Clint shouted. Just as he'd hoped, he attracted Hobbes's attention just long enough for him to see he'd lost another two men.

"I should say the same to you, Adams!" Hobbes shouted. "Because this place is about to get blown off the goddamn map!"

When he said that, Hobbes took on a wild look that made him seem more like an animal than a man. He also nodded up toward the second floor of the building across the street from the marshal's office. As Clint looked there as well, he saw three windows open and three men leaning outside with rifles in their hands.

Apparently, the men in that camp hadn't been Hobbes's only source of reinforcements.

FORTY-FOUR

Lyssa turned to get a look at the windows opening above her as her ears were ringing from the gunshots that had already been fired. Just as she was about to raise her arm and take a shot at one of the riflemen, she felt something clamp around her elbow and pull her almost hard enough to take her off her feet.

Another arm wrapped around her like a band of steel and soon Hobbes's breath was gusting against her face.

"Just sit real still, darlin'," Hobbes whispered as he jabbed his gun into her ribs. "Maybe you'll live long enough to have some fun with me a little later."

Lyssa squirmed and fought, but Hobbes was too strong for her.

Clint rushed into the street as the riflemen started firing down at him and the lawmen. One of the deputies returned fire and got close enough to force one of the riflemen back. Without breaking his stride, Clint aimed at the second floor of that building and squeezed his trigger.

The rifleman in the middle window fell straight back like a metal target.

Shifting his aim a bit to the right, Clint steadied his arm

and fired his last shot. For a moment, he thought he'd missed the man in that window. Then, the rifleman slouched forward, dropped his gun and fell out of the window all the way to the street.

Clint wasted no time in snapping open his pistol, emptying the cylinder and reloading it. All the while, as his hands went through those motions, he prayed he would finish while there was still time to make a difference.

"You had your chance, Earp!" Hobbes shouted as he held Lyssa in front of him. "Now drop that shotgun or you'll get to watch another one of your little helpers die!"

With his face still bearing its ever-present scowl, Virgil chucked away the shotgun and stood up straight. "All this fuss to take down a one-armed marshal. You must be real proud of yourself."

Thumbing back the hammer and shifting his pistol to aim at Virgil instead of Lyssa, Hobbes smirked and said, "I'll let you know how I feel once you're dead."

The moment she felt the gun was no longer pressed against her side, Lyssa drove her elbow into Hobbes's ribs and ducked down low.

Virgil took advantage of the moment by snapping his right hand down to pluck the pistol from its holster and bring it up in a smooth motion. He pulled his trigger without blinking and sent a bullet straight through the side of Hobbes's neck.

Hobbes let out the cry of a wounded animal as he staggered to one side and fought to bring his arm up again. Before he could take a shot at Virgil, Lyssa was throwing herself at him again. This time, she lashed out with both fists clasped together and slammed them into Hobbes's gut.

"Goddammit, Lyssa, get the hell away from him!" Virgil shouted.

Suddenly, another shot cracked through the air. This wasn't fired by Virgil or Hobbes, but instead came from Clint's modified Colt and caught Hobbes in the forearm. It wasn't a killing shot, but it was the best one he could manage with Lyssa standing so close to his target. It was also enough to spin Hobbes away from Lyssa and get him more or less in the open.

Hobbes gritted his teeth and set his sights upon Virgil. His arm came up despite being wounded and he managed to sight along the barrel of his gun.

Staring right down that barrel, Virgil took aim and squeezed his trigger. His gun bucked against his palm and delivered a round straight into Hobbes's chest.

Jerking at the impact of that bullet, Hobbes coughed and swayed on his feet. Although he still fought to aim his gun at Virgil, he no longer had the strength to do so. His arm swung down to hang limply at his side and then he collapsed in the street.

Clint stepped forward and kept his gun aimed at Hobbes. He kept his Colt pointed at the man until he could walk up and kick the gun out of Hobbes's reach. "You all right?" he asked Lyssa.

He got his answer in the form of a hug that nearly took Clint off his feet. Lyssa wrapped her arms around him and held on tightly. For a few seconds, it seemed as though she was never going to let go of him. Then she eased up her grip, took a step back and surveyed the street.

Bodies were strewn everywhere, but most of them were the gunmen that had accompanied Hobbes. A few deputies were sprawled in the dirt, but most of the lawmen were either already back on their feet and tending to the ones who were still on the ground.

"Is this finally over?" Lyssa asked.

Virgil walked up to them and holstered his gun. "There's always loose ends to tie up, but I'd say this particular end was tied up nicely."

Letting out a breath, Clint said, "You're getting a bit slow on the draw, Virgil."

"You should have seen me in my prime," Virgil replied with the widest grin he'd shown since Clint had arrived in Colton.

Lyssa rushed over to the older man and gave him a hug as well. When she took a look at him, she found him glaring at her sternly.

"What's the matter?" she asked.

"You were told to stay back," Virgil replied. "Maybe then you wouldn't have been taken like that."

"Can we argue about this some other time?" she asked.

After a bit, Virgil nodded. "Another loose end, huh? I think I can handle that."

Clint was about to start tending to one of the wounded deputies when he saw a thick hand extended toward him.

"I don't have the words, Clint," Virgil said. "But thanks."

Shaking Virgil's hand, Clint replied, "Those are all the words you need."

FORTY-FIVE

The building across the street from the marshal's office had been cleared out hours ago. Actually, the few people inside of it had been rounded up, herded into a room and tied up so they would be out of the way when Hobbes's riflemen took their positions. Being the leader of those gunmen, Jeff Conway had seen to that himself.

As he rushed down the stairs, he could hear the hostages shouting from inside the room where they were locked up. If Jeff hadn't caught a bullet in the arm when Clint had fired up at his window a few minutes ago, he might have been in the mood to kill a few of those damn screaming hostages.

But Jeff was in no mood for that. He could still see Clint staring right up at him, picking him out of the others and making sure to kill him first. The more he thought about it, the more he hated that goddamn Adams.

Jeff grabbed his wounded arm to keep the blood from spilling out of him too quickly. He then rushed to the back of the building and hurried out to where the riflemen's horses were waiting. Since none of the other men had made it, Jeff took the fastest of the three horses and pulled himself into the saddle.

Part of him wished there were enough deputies left to try and stop him.

Another part of him wished he could see Clint's face one last time so he could put a bullet through it.

The biggest part of him just wanted to get the hell out of Colton so he could heal up and kill Clint some other time.

Another loose end.

Watch for

SNAKEBITE CREEK

299th novel in the exciting GUNSMITH series
from Jove

Coming in November!

J. R. ROBERTS
THE GUNSMITH